Amusing Miss Austen

ANGELA PEARSE

For my fellow Jane Austen fans

PART ONE

Ashbury Manor Is Let

Chapter 1

Steventon, Summer 1796

It stands to reason that if a young lady cavorts with a young man in a barn at midnight, her chemise will be full of hay.

A flurry of pale strands fell as I valiantly shook them out as best I could, kissed him goodbye, and hastened back to the house. Finger-combing still more hay out of my mussy hair, I replaited it before slipping in the side door—the small one we didn't lock because the key was lost. Our maid, Mary, might notice the odd bit of hay lying about tomorrow. But she was discreet and would sweep it up without commenting to Papa.

Only when I was treading lightly across the floorboards in the upstairs hallway and safely back in my room did I breathe a sigh of relief. I swore to myself that this was the last time I'd see him. But I knew I did not mean it because I loved sneaking out at night to meet with Samuel Green—it was even more thrilling than the cavorting.

* * *

'You need to be more careful, Fliss,' my sister, Harriet, said the next morning at breakfast. She looked down her shapely nose at me. 'Aunt drinks two cups of chamomile tea before bed, which means usage of the chamber pot throughout the night and curtain twitching. It's only a matter of time before she sees you creeping out or back in. She'll tell Papa immediately, and then you're done for.'

I paused in buttering my roll. *Blast, I hadn't considered that.* Harriet—two years older and sensible, whereas I was impulsive—was correct as usual. Mrs Snelling lived right next door to our house. And the side door I used was in full view of her first-floor bedroom window. We called her 'Aunt', but she wasn't related. She was a neighbour with a strong interest in our upbringing (and also our widowed father).

Nervously, I eyed the dining room door through which Papa could suddenly appear. Indeed, his footsteps sounded forthwith in the passageway, and I said in a low whisper, 'Yes, all right. But can we not talk about it here?'

Harriet pursed her lips and said nothing further, taking a delicate sip of tea, while I busied myself with the jam. Charles Blackburn, looking spruce in one of his own grey suits, strode into the room. He was a tailor of some merit in the village and employed several apprentices.

'Morning, Papa,' we chorused.

'Morning, girls,' he replied, seating himself at the table. 'Ah, good, you've started. I'm rather late this morning. Luckily, I don't have my first customer until ten o'clock.'

'Are you quite well, Papa?' asked Harriet with concern. 'You look tired.'

Indeed, Papa's ruddy complexion had a distinct pallor.

He rubbed his face distractedly. 'Yes, thank you, Harriet. Something disturbed me in the early hours of the morning, and I was unable to fall back to sleep.'

'Perhaps it was a ghost roaming the hallway?' she offered, and I kicked her ankle smartly under the table. Harriet flinched, drawing her leg underneath the chair, and flashed me an evil grin.

He sighed. 'Yes, maybe it was, of a sort. Your mother has been on my mind lately. It's her birthday next week.'

Our collective gaze fell upon the life-size portrait that was occupying pride of place on the wall. Adelaide Blackburn, the beautiful silent member of our family, who was always in attendance at breakfast but who could be trusted not to breathe a word of our conversations. Papa kept her memory alive by telling us stories of how she'd captured his heart with her exuberance, quick wit, and charm. There was no other for him, and he missed her dearly. She plagued his dreams and was often in his thoughts, but most especially for her birthday, their anniversary, and Christmas.

Harriet was pragmatic, fair-haired, and blue-eyed. But I'd inherited my mother's exuberance, dark hair, and brown eyes; and at times, seeing me reminded Papa acutely of his loss. He'd told me under no circumstances should I feel to blame, but I still did. I had from the time when I was five, when I'd overheard a forthright female relation tell her friend that the time of my mother's death and the time of my birth were one and the same. 'Oh, how ghastly for the poor child—to have killed her own mother!' exclaimed the friend with a gloved hand to her mouth. So from then on, I was haunted by her too—haunted by guilt.

The three of us continued with our respective breakfasts in silence until Mary appeared and bobbed, saying that we had a visitor.

'We're in the middle of breakfast, Mary,' said Papa with a frown. 'Who is it?'

'Mrs Snelling, sir. She said she had important news to share.'

Harriet repaid me with a swift kick to my ankle, and I grimaced at her.

'Of course it's important,' said Papa with a sigh. He tolerated Aunt's penchant for gossip and was always polite to her (but it was perhaps why he hadn't returned her subtle overtures towards him). 'Well, you may as well show her in so we can hear her news. Please make a fresh pot of tea and bring another cup.'

'Yes, sir.' Mary took up the flowered china teapot and hurried out of the room. I groaned inwardly. This was it, my reckoning. She'd tinkled and seen me and was now going to tell on me to Papa.

We didn't have long to wait. A light step was heard in the hallway, and in she came. For a woman in her early forties, Prudence Snelling, I had to admit, cut a distinctive figure. A widow of five years, her dress was elegant rather than fashionable; and her features, while not conventionally striking, were expressive. Her sharp eyes, made sharper by her grey-streaked brown hair pulled back tightly in a bun, missed nothing. After greeting Papa with a bow, she turned to Harriet and me and appeared to be in possession of some kind of restless excitement. Mary reappeared with the teapot, and I took it from her.

'Would you care for some tea, Aunt? It's freshly made,' I said, remembering my manners.

'Thank you, dear, just half a cup. I shan't stay long,' she replied. 'But I've just come from the post shop, and I had to tell you immediately. Such news!'

'Is it to do with the delivery of muslin from London?'

asked Papa, sounding bored already. 'If so, we already know about that.'

But Aunt, undeterred, put down her cup after a cursory sip and leaned forward, her light-blue eyes sparkling. 'No, something much more exciting than muslin. Ashbury Manor is let! To a young gentleman from London. He will be taking it up within a few days. I have it on good account that he is wealthy too, five thousand a year.'

'Five thousand!' breathed Harriet. 'Why on earth does he want to live here?'

'What's wrong with here?' I asked, feeling protective of our little patch. 'Steventon may not be London, but we still have enjoyable diversions, and the air is much fresher.'

'I just meant there is so much more in the way of entertainment and company ...'

Aunt sniffed. 'I'm sure that when I visited my sister in London last month, I wished to be gone after a few days. The constant bustle is tiresome. *He*, no doubt, wishes to experience the peace and tranquillity of the English countryside. However, I believe his family originates from Wales.'

'Wales! Then we shall have to call him Taffy,' I quipped. 'You know, after the rhyme "Taffy was a Welshman, Taffy was a thief, Taffy came to my house and stole a leg of beef".'

Harriet snorted, and even Aunt looked amused.

Papa had remained silent throughout this exchange but now said thoughtfully, 'I suppose I should pay a visit as soon as he arrives.'

'For what purpose?' I asked blithely.

Aunt clicked her tongue. 'Really, Felicity, for an intelligent young woman, you can be oblivious at times. This is a remarkable opportunity. He would make a fine match for either you or Harriet.'

'Have you seen him?' I questioned her.

'Well, no ... But I'm sure he's amiable.'

'For all we know, he may have all manner of ailments,' I scoffed, folding my arms decisively. 'I'm not marrying a Welshman with a limp or excessive nose hair!'

Harriet snickered. 'Me neither!'

Aunt shook her head. 'Fussy girls! Then, pray, who else will you marry? For I have racked my brain, and there is no one I can think of in the village who might be suitable.'

It was on the tip of my tongue to mention Samuel Green, who had reiterated his intention to marry me last night. But I knew Papa would not approve of a farmer's son with hearty passions, but no money. It was why I was sneaking around at night.

So I said nothing. Perhaps this Welshman would be rich,

handsome, and agreeable *and* fall in love with either me or my sister. Stranger things had happened. They didn't usually occur in Steventon, but we could all hope for the best.

'Visit him if you like, Papa. I, for one, should be glad to make his acquaintance,' I said.

'Oho, now you change your tune. Was it the five thousand a year that did it?' teased Papa. I began to protest that it wasn't about the money, but meeting new people, but he silenced me with his hand.

'No, no, it's settled. I'll visit the day after he arrives. Thank you, Mrs Snelling, for letting us know.'

She inclined her head towards him and looked pleased with herself. A peacock preening its feathers came to mind.

'I shall visit Jane this morning and see if she's heard anything. One of her brothers may have met him,' I ventured to Harriet.

'Oh yes, do.'

Aunt's expression tightened. 'I'm not sure you should spend so much time with Miss Austen. Her father wishes her to concentrate on studying and abstain from frivolity, which tends to happen when you visit.'

I felt a bit affronted at that. 'I'm not sure what he means. I am always perfectly well behaved.'

'Hmm,' said Aunt. 'May I remind you of the tea-, pie-, and cake-buying incident?'

Harriet giggled as my cheeks turned a light shade of pink.

A month ago, Jane had dared me to dress in her brother Henry's clothes and don his hat. The urge to do something outrageous had overcome us, and we'd walked into town arm in arm, and she waited outside while I bought a packet of tea from an unsuspecting shopkeeper. The disguise had worked so well that, buoyed with confidence, I'd bounced into another shop and bought a couple of pork pies, then into another to purchase some cakes. Giggling like mad things, we'd run back to her house with my purchases to devour them in secret. But unfortunately, someone told Mr Austen that Jane had been gallivanting around the village with a young man unchaperoned. He'd questioned her, and the story came out. I'd had to swear on my life to never wear boy's clothes again before he would allow me to visit her.

'At least Jane knows how to have fun, unlike some people,' I muttered under my breath.

***

The Austens lived in a rectory slightly out of town. As the sky threatened rain, I rode over there on our buggy horse, George, whom I'd named after the king. George was apt to get sidetracked and often paid no heed to my commands, so in truth, it took me a longer time than if I'd walked.

When I finally arrived at their flint-and-brick home, the first drops of rain were falling. I left George tied up under a side shelter, happily munching on some grass. Their maid, Amy, showed me in; and Mr Austen poked his head out of his library as I entered and told me Jane was upstairs. He was not unfriendly, but I gladly took my leave, not wanting to be caught up in a conversation that would lead to a sermon. As a respected clergyman and teacher, he did scare me a little; and from what Aunt had said to me at breakfast, I gathered he had been in discussion with her about applying a firmer hand. I had to indeed be more careful as Harriet had warned. Otherwise, I might find myself packed off to Lord knows where to be a governess. It was a sobering thought.

Climbing the stairs, I made my way along the hall to Jane's 'parlour', which she shared with her elder sister, Cassandra. It was in fact an adjoining bedroom that had recently been converted so they had extra space to entertain. The latter was currently visiting their brother Edward and his family in Kent, so she wasn't present.

I knocked gently and went in to find Jane sitting at the table with her writing slope. She was penning something, a letter I assumed.

She looked up, her bright hazel eyes large in her heart-shaped face, which was prettily framed with curls. 'Flissy! How lovely to see you!' she cried, dropping her quill and jumping up to hug me. She was taller than me, so I had to tiptoe. 'Pooh, you smell of horse! Did you ride over on George?'

'I did,' I said, gladly removing my pelisse along with my gloves and bonnet, for the parlour let in the morning sun, and the room was warm. A spare chair became my clothes rack; and I looked around, taking in the brown carpet, painted shelves, and striped curtains. Though scantily furnished, it was a cosy space, and I wished Harriet and I had one like it. But to do so, we would have to share a bed, and I valued my privacy too much for that.

Jane bade me to sit on the sofa. 'Are you writing to Cassie?' I asked curiously, watching her blot and slide her paper into the desk. Her letters to her sister were always quite private, though she also wrote to me if the weather was inclement; and I found her epistles witty entertainment indeed, especially during winter, when it was so dull in the village.

'Yes, I am, but I can finish it later. I was about to have luncheon. Shall I ring for some sandwiches?' she said, successfully diverting my attention to my stomach.

'Yes please.'

After that was arranged, she focused her attention on my visit. 'So what brings you to my parlour, my pretty?' She put on a witchy voice and made as if to claw my face, and I laughed, batting her hands away.

'I wanted to tell you some exciting news. Well, it's exciting in the face of nothing else going on.'

'Oooh, do tell.'

'Ashbury Manor has apparently been let to a young gentleman from London.'

Jane's expression immediately lost its air of expectation. 'Oh, that. I knew about *that* last week.'

'What? How?'

'Well, Ashbury's only a half mile from here. And the road has been busy with carriages and carts with an awful lot of furniture going up to the house, including a grandfather clock, an inlaid sideboard, and some jolly nice rugs ...' My eyes must've glazed over at this point as she continued hastily. 'Anyway, Father chatted with one of the carriage drivers who'd stopped outside our gate for a smoke, and he quite cheerfully imparted that a Mr Evan Pringle would be taking over the lease.'

My eyebrows rose at this. 'We didn't know his name, only that he may originally be from Wales.'

Jane nodded emphatically. 'Yes, he is, and he has a—'

Our sandwiches and a pot of tea on a tray arrived just

then, so there was some delay before she could continue.

'You were saying?' I prompted. 'Please don't tell me the missing word is "limp".'

Jane snorted. 'Limp! No, I was about to say he has a *friend* who is also to stay with him. By all accounts, wealthy and single too.'

'Good Lord, two rich eligible gentlemen gracing us with their presence! Let us hope they're amiable.' I took a large bite of my ham, tomato, and mustard sandwich, enjoying the tasty flavours. The Austens kept their own sty and vegetable gardens, so the food was always excellent.

'Of his amiability, I can't comment,' said Jane.

'What is his friend's name?'

'I can't comment on that either because I don't have it.'

'Oh, so we only have half a story. We're going to have to make the rest up!'

'Well, that's easily done,' she said with a wry smile. 'For a start, I would imagine single men of good fortune must be wanting wives. And Lord knows there are enough unattached women in this village for them to take their pick.'

'You sound like Aunt. She's practically frothing at the mouth for Harriet or me to marry one of them.'

'But I thought you were promised to a certain Mr

Green?' Jane said in a teasing tone.

'You know that won't be happening. It's just frolics.'

'Tell me the latest about your dalliance. I have space left in my letter, and I need to liven it up since it is so dull. Cassie can cut that bit out after she's read it, and you know she won't say anything.'

So I told her, as I always did, because she was interested and she was my trusted friend. Jane had a way of listening with her whole being, absorbed in every word; she was like a cat with catnip when it came to interactions between the sexes. And she always gave excellent advice. For all her sheltered life, she was much wiser in the ways of men than I, probably because she had six brothers.

Chapter 2

Two weeks later, I was preparing for the summer assembly in the village hall. It wasn't a formal affair, so I didn't need to wear my best white muslin. But still, I dithered over my meagre selection of second bests, a blue and a green, which were already out of fashion. Papa simply couldn't afford to keep up with the ever-changing styles that came out of London, and hidden from society here in Steventon, it wasn't fair of us to demand them. So Harriet and I made do. But still, it would have been nice to have a selection of more than two evening dresses.

Sighing, I plucked out the green, shimmied into it, and attempted to pile my hair and pin it without much success.

'Here, let me.' Harriet pushed me down in front of the dressing table mirror. She'd been lounging on my bed, waiting for me to get ready, absorbed in her latest Gothic romance novel, *The Castle of Otranto*. Jane had lent it to her from her father's library.

'How's the book?' I asked.

'Excellent,' said Harriet, curling and pinning with dexterity. 'It's so spooky I daren't read it at night.'

I shuddered. 'I don't know how you can read it at all. I'm surprised Mr Austen has it in his library.'

'He's beginning to cultivate quite the Gothic collection, what with Ann Radcliffe and William Beckford too. There, what do you think?'

She held up a small mirror behind my head so I could see the full effect. My unruly mane had been tamed into a sleek coiffured style.

'Wonders! You've made me look so presentable I might even receive a dance or two.'

Harriet smiled at me in the mirror. 'I would've thought that was par for the course with Mr Green in attendance. Isn't that why you're wearing his colour?'

'He will be there, but we might not speak or dance much. We never do at these things. I've cautioned him against overfamiliarity. I would be surprised if he even looked directly at me.'

'It's a strange connection you two have, I'm sure.' Harriet shook her head. 'What's the point of being practically engaged if you can't enjoy each other's company in public?'

Because we enjoy each other's company much more in private, I thought. Aloud, I said, 'Because we are not practically engaged. Anyway, never mind about me. I hear Mr Pringle will be attending tonight. You are bound to catch his attention.'

I surveyed her with an admiring eye. Harriet was looking resplendent in peach silk, a thin band of gold twined through her hair, and our mother's pearl drop earrings completing the elegant effect.

Her eyes met mine in the mirror. 'Do you think so?'

I nodded confidently. 'If he doesn't ask you to dance, I shall consider him a fool.'

Harriet giggled. 'He may ask you to dance, Fliss, and be so charming you'll have to consider him otherwise.'

I grinned at her. 'I'll keep an open mind if that eventuality occurs.'

* * *

The dance was in full swing when Papa, Aunt, Harriet, and I arrived. The hall was a crush of people; and the heat, music, and clatter of stamping feet made my head swim after the quiet cool of the country lanes. Spotting Jane standing by the window, I pushed my way over to her.

'Flissy! Finally!' We clasped hands and kissed cheeks. 'Why are you so late?' she scolded. 'There's already been two sets.'

'Aunt made us wait in her parlour while she searched for a "misplaced" glove. She likes to be fashionably late,' I explained, quelling the urge to roll my eyes. I searched the throng of dancers, looking for Samuel's flaxen hair but couldn't see him amongst them.

'Have you been up?'

Jane inclined her head. 'Just with my brother for the first. But see who's he talking to now.'

She moved back slightly, and farther along the wall, I glimpsed Jane's elder brother Henry in conversation with Samuel. My heart skipped a beat as he looked over, his eyes meeting mine. He gave a slow nod, and his gaze roved over my dress approvingly. My cheeks flushed, and I wished I'd worn the blue so it didn't look so obvious I was thinking about him. A dressing error on my part. I returned the nod and attempted to breathe steadily, which was difficult since Harriet had laced my stays overly tight. Another dressing error.

Jane squeezed my hand. 'Don't look now, but a likely prospect approaches. Act natural.'

We proceeded to confer about the inclement weather of late when a hesitant voice came over my right shoulder.

'Miss Blackburn?'

I turned to find short, stocky Will Hayes, one of Papa's apprentices, before me. His complexion was typically pale and freckled, but on this occasion, his cheeks were fiery red and competing with his ginger hair. He must have been dancing to look so exerted.

'If you are free, would you stand up with me for the next dance?' he asked somewhat breathlessly.

I could see no reason why not. 'I'd be delighted. Thank you, Mr Hayes,' I said with a smile.

'The pleasure is all mine.' He bowed abruptly and moved off to wait a few feet away.

'Will is overly eager,' remarked Jane, looking amused. 'I'd watch out there.'

'Oh, it's just one dance. He won't commandeer me for another if I do not wish it.' My eyes slid to Samuel, his back to me now and posture stiff as if assiduously ignoring me. Had he witnessed Will's invitation? Surely, he wasn't professing jealousy? He was ten times better-looking than Will Hayes, and he knew it. I sighed. Perhaps I should dance a couple of alternate sets with Samuel. I liked him a lot and didn't want to cause offence if he was feeling insecure.

I was about to suggest to Jane that she talk to her brother about talking to Samuel so he could ask me. But the call came to take our places for the next dance. Will proffered his arm and led me away, so I didn't have the opportunity.

The rhythm of the music and the energy of the boisterous crowd lifted my spirits, and I laughed with pleasure as I clapped and stamped and whirled around. Anyone who was caught up in it couldn't fail to be stirred—unless you weren't one of the ones dancing. Then it was very much a matter of living vicariously through others, which was what had happened to my sister, I realised with some dismay. Harriet's beauty was too intimidating, and the men in attendance feared rejection, so she hadn't been asked to dance. Her face was one of stoic misery as she watched on. Papa had gone off somewhere while Aunt was talking animatedly to her friend and not including Harriet at all. She was completely alone. I grabbed Will's arm on the turn.

'Would you be so kind as to ask my sister to stand up for the next?' I said.

His smile faltered, and I understood that he had intended to ask me again. But this would put a stop to that and help Harriet.

'Please, as a favour to me?' I implored.

He nodded before twirling me away from him. As he did so, my relief at having saved Harriet from wallflower status changed to surprise when I caught sight of Samuel dancing with Jane farther up the line. He must have asked her, or his brother had told him to. A knot of discomfort worked its way into the tight cavity beneath my stays as I observed them. Samuel was an excellent dancer, and Jane was light on her feet. They made a good match. He caught my eye as he held her hand on the promenade and grinned cheekily at my disapproving expression. I couldn't believe it. He'd planned it so I'd get equally jealous, and it had worked. The conniving fool!

The music ended with a flourish, and we all clapped enthusiastically. I bowed to Will, then gestured to Harriet, and he nodded. We made our way over to her, and he dutifully asked her for the next dance. I sighed in relief, seeing her face brighten as she nodded her assent.

I was fanning myself against the wall, Harriet having gone off with Will to the supper room to fetch us cold drinks, when Jane appeared. She was smiling widely, which was no surprise, for Samuel was the handsomest man in the room. A greater determination to dance with him rose in me seeing her pleasure. I wanted to see her happily matched, of course I did—just not with Samuel. I was playing a risky game with him. If I wasn't careful, he'd lose interest and ditch me for someone else more appreciative, like Jane. I needed to show him I wasn't too proud to be seen with a farmer's son in public, though there was a certain matter we needed to discuss before I could assent to marriage.

Jane grasped my hands; hers were slightly moist, and her curls were damp on her forehead. She opened her mouth to say something. But before she could, there was a kind of murmured rustling in the crowd, and heads started turning towards the door.

'What's happening?' I asked, and she craned her neck to see.

'He's here! Mr Pringle—he's arrived,' she replied excitedly.

'Where?' Cursing my lack of height, I stood on my tiptoes and looked over, but all I could discern was a sea of heads. Then a few people shifted. A man, a tall austere man with dark hair and a handsome face, came into view. He was standing by the entrance, surveying everyone with a haughty expression.

'Gracious. Is that him?' I whispered to Jane, holding up my fan so our conversation would be private.

Jane whipped up her own fan. 'Oh no, that's Mr Pringle's friend, Mr Fitzroy,' she whispered back. 'Apparently, he's even richer.'

'Mr Stonyface's money doesn't seem to have made him very happy,' I remarked, lowering my fan to peer at him. 'He looks like he would rather be anywhere else at this present moment.'

Jane tittered. '*Mr Stonyface*. Now that is an unfortunate nickname to incur.'

'Mr Pringle looks ten times more amiable.' I could now observe his fair-haired friend who was busily making the acquaintance of mothers and daughters, no doubt eager to have him round for tea. Slightly shorter than Mr Stonyface and not as overtly handsome, still, he exhibited a cheerful and pleasant demeanour, which that other gentleman sorely lacked.

'Felicity!' Aunt appeared, and we snapped our fans shut and stood to attention. 'Where's Harriet?' she demanded.

'With Will Hayes,' I replied. 'They went to the supper room—'

Aunt clicked her tongue. 'Will Hayes? No, no, that won't do. She has to come and meet Mr Pringle this instant. And you too, of course, dear.'

Jane and I exchanged smirks.

After a few minutes, Harriet and Will appeared. Aunt immediately took her elbow and herded her towards the front of the room, leaving behind a bewildered Mr Hayes clutching her drink and his. Jane and I trailed along behind, sharing my glass of chilled wine. It appeared we were about to become acquainted with Mr Pringle and his dour friend.

When we approached, Mr Pringle was speaking to Papa about needing a new suit; he seemed to be describing what he wanted in great detail. Papa was nodding and saying things like 'That won't be any trouble' and 'I have those exact buttons'. I assumed Aunt had seen a window of opportunity for an introduction and hastened away while they were talking.

Papa turned and saw our posse. 'Ah, Mr Pringle, may I introduce my daughters, Harriet and Felicity Blackburn.' We exchanged bows.

'There is also Jane, Papa,' I said, pushing her forward slightly.

'And Jane Austen, Reverend Austen's daughter.'

Mr Pringle smiled widely, showing off a good set of straight white teeth. 'Hello, Miss Austen. We meet again.' His voice had a strong Welsh lilt that was not unpleasing.

'Mr Pringle,' she said, bowing.

We all turned to her. 'Mr Pringle's daily rides take him past our house, and he's stopped in once or twice to see Father. The other day, he stayed for Sunday luncheon,' she explained.

'A delicious roast hogget it was too! And you and your brothers were most excellent company.'

I could see by Aunt's frown that she was becoming annoyed that Mr Pringle was paying more attention to Jane than Harriet.

'How long do you plan to stay in Steventon, Mr Pringle?' I interjected hastily. 'Do you not miss London?'

'No, not at all,' he said, smiling at me. 'In fact, I'm rather enjoying exchanging birdsong for bustle. London does drain one so with its constant demands.'

'Exactly what I think, Mr Pringle!' exclaimed Aunt. 'I

think you'll find Steventon and our small, but lively dances much more to your taste.'

Throughout this exchange, Mr Fitzroy was standing off to the side, within earshot, but not bothering to make our acquaintance. But now he had no choice but to be drawn in with Mr Pringle's next comment. 'I'm sure I shall. But I'm afraid my friend Mr Fitzroy here wholeheartedly disagrees with me. He detests country dances and had to be persuaded to come tonight on pain of death. Didn't you, Max?' Mr Pringle said, looking round at him with a grin.

Mr Fitzroy nodded but declined to respond. Clearly, he thought we were too far below him in rank to even speak to!

I found myself wishing he would take himself off back to London immediately so he didn't have to spoil our fun with his disdain.

'Perhaps if you danced, Mr Fitzroy, you might find the assembly more to your liking?' I said, unable to help myself.

Immediately, his piercing gaze was upon me, and I noticed how unusually blue his eyes were. Coupled with his handsomeness, I couldn't help but feel somewhat affected as he stared at me for what felt like an eternity without speaking. Then he averted his eyes and said gruffly, 'I never dance, unless my partner is well known to me.'

'But how will you make friends if you hide yourself away

in the corner?' I persisted.

I'd obviously struck a nerve as Mr Fitzroy's countenance darkened, and his lips tightened.

'If you'll excuse me,' he said, bowed, and strode off outside.

I was left open-mouthed at his rudeness, though my comment had been impertinent, I supposed. But still. What an unpleasant man! He and Mr Pringle were like chalk and cheese.

The latter had, in an attempt to smooth over his friend's frosty departure, turned his attention to Harriet. 'Miss Blackburn, I'd be delighted if you would partner me for the next dance, if you are not otherwise engaged?'

Harriet started, 'Oh, actually ...' But I shook my head at her, behind his back. Will could wait, for goodness' sake! This was a much better offer. 'Thank you, I'd be delighted,' she said. Mr Pringle offered her his arm, and they disappeared into the throng.

'Well!' said Aunt, looking mightily pleased at the outcome of her introduction. 'Let us pray that he'll find Harriet to be another merit of the countryside.'

Jane and I, not having partners, went outside for a breather. Beneath one of the windows round the back of the hall was a small wooden bench, and we sank onto it. I, for one, was glad to escape the confines of the crowded, stuffy tallow-scented room. It had also become tainted with the presence of that rude gentleman, who had seemed to suck all the enjoyment out of the evening for me.

'What did you think of him, Jane? Mr Stonyface?' I asked, expecting immediate agreement, for we usually shared the same opinion on most things.

'His behaviour was awkward,' she said after hesitating for a moment. 'But I think that was because he was shy.'

'Shy!' I let out a hoot of laughter. 'You're a kind judge to be sure. I thought him the most impolite person I've ever met!'

'Hush, Flissy.' She peered into the bushes that surrounded the back of the hall. 'He came outside, did he not? He may overhear.'

'Excellent.' I folded my arms and leaned back against the wall, looking up at the few twinkling stars in the night sky. 'I hope he does and is more considerate in future.'

Jane glanced at me. 'So you wish to see him again?'

'No, I meant—'

Whatever I meant was quickly silenced by Jane as she put a finger to her lips. Two figures had appeared at the corner of the building in proximity to where we sat in the darkness, and from the light of the window, they were easily recognisable as Mr Pringle and his disagreeable friend.

Mr Pringle was expounding on his enjoyment of dancing

with Harriet, while Mr Fitzroy grunted something I couldn't quite hear. 'Come now, Max, you must agree there are a number of pretty girls in attendance.'

'No, I disagree entirely,' said he. 'You were dancing with the only tolerable one. As for the rest of her party, the piglets running around in the Austens' sty are more attractive.'

I stiffened in shock. Did he actually just compare us to pigs and find us wanting? Any notion I'd had about giving Mr Fitzroy a second chance was completely extinguished and replaced by anger. If Jane hadn't been gripping me firmly by the arm, I may have leapt up, rushed over, and pummelled him.

The rest of their conversation flowed past my ears, but I didn't bother to listen. Debrief finished, they moved off back inside the hall.

'Now surely you must change your opinion of him? You cannot stick up for a man who says he finds piglets more attractive than us!' I hissed.

Jane shook her head and said soberly, 'Yes, I think you are right. Well, if he has such a preference for our farmyard animals, I'll have to ask Father to formally introduce him. Oink oink!'

We collapsed into giggles.

Chapter 3

Despite Jane and I laughing about it, I still felt the sting of Mr Fitzroy's insult and couldn't help but feel offended. I wasn't vain like some women, far from it. But for some reason, him not thinking I was attractive irked me severely. Who did he think he was? I longed to make him eat his words and thoroughly choke on them.

Leaving Jane to converse with Harriet, I went in search of Samuel and eventually found him leaning against the wall in the supper room, consuming a plate of ham.

'Miss Blackburn.' He started to bow, but I cut him off.

'Forget that. I want you to dance with me,' I said impatiently.

Confusion crossed his face. 'But I thought we weren't going to—'

'Do you want to dance with me or not? If not, I'll find Mr Hayes and flutter my eyelashes. I'm sure he will be glad to dance another ...'

Samuel quickly deposited the remainder of his plate of ham on a nearby chair. 'No need for that,' he said, proffering his arm. 'If you require a dance partner, I'm happy to assist.'

Relief flooded through me. Why I was so desperate for Samuel to dance with me, I hardly knew. But I supposed it was something to do with not wanting to be a wallflower after Mr Stonyface's insult; it would be like he was right. I needed him to see that I was desirable and desired no less by the handsomest man there (excluding himself). As Samuel and I walked into the main room, I couldn't resist a surreptitious glance around but did not see Mr Fitzroy. Maybe he'd left, having found the occasion too beneath his contempt to bear any longer.

Harriet and Jane were looking on from the sidelines with undisguised curiosity as Samuel and I lined up. But then something extraordinary happened—Mr Pringle swooped in and asked Harriet to dance again. I couldn't believe my eyes, and I saw Aunt notice it too and nudge Papa. Mr Pringle asking Harriet to dance once was polite, but twice, and of his own accord, meant that he was obviously taken with her.

Harriet moved into place beside me, and as the dance began, the look of pleasure on her face as she was twirled by Mr Pringle signified she was immensely flattered at being singled out by him. Even better was the look of displeasure I caught on Mr Fitzroy's face as he appeared in my line of sight. Hah, he had not left after all!

At first, I thought his glower was because Mr Pringle had partnered Harriet. But after several turns, I realised his unwavering disdainful stare was firmly centred on *me*. It was petty, but I felt a small thrill and was sure to make the most of Samuel's attention by gazing at him adoringly and acting like I was truly enamoured. It was extremely satisfying.

* * *

Yet as much as I despised him, try as I might, I could not get those penetrating blue eyes of Mr Fitzroy's out of my head for several days afterwards. They appeared without warning, such as when I was idly brushing my hair at the dressing table or looking out the window. They even appeared once when I was stirring my cup of tea. I had to blink twice at the sudden image of unyielding eyes staring back at me in the swirling brown liquid. It was most disconcerting. What could it mean? I had no interest in forming a connection with the man. After what he'd said at the dance, I could hardly bear to be in the same room with him. Indeed, being within five steps of him made my skin prickle.

Harriet had no such issues with his likeable friend. It was all "Mr Pringle this" and "Mr Pringle that" for days afterwards. To be fair, Mr Pringle was far superior to Mr Stonyface, and he'd asked her to dance twice. So I didn't begrudge her speaking of him so emphatically. It was nice to see her happy. However, as a week or so passed and she didn't receive a letter with his intention to call, I wondered if he did indeed have as much admiration for her as we'd all thought. Even Jane was surprised at his lack of communication and declared it most odd. We conjectured that he must be preoccupied with some business matter or have gone away to London. She said she had been awakened by a fast-moving carriage in the early hours of the morning three days past, and perhaps it had been him? It was all presumption on our part.

Meanwhile, poor Harriet bore his slight well and stoically as I knew she would. Never let it be said that a Blackburn girl crumbled under the pressure of waiting for a gentleman to write!

But after another week passed without seeing hide nor hair of the fine gentleman, it was too much, and she cracked.

'Let us go into Overton for ribbons,' she said to me rather brightly one morning at breakfast. 'I need some new ones.'

Now walking was one of my favourite pastimes. But it was a two-hour round trip, and with the hotter weather we'd been having lately, Overton was a destination best reached by buggy. However, George would be a horror to manage if a journey of that length was foisted upon him without due preparation (namely a large bag of oats and much mollycoddling).

'Can we not visit the haberdasher's here in Steventon?' I asked. 'It is so much closer.'

To my dismay, Harriet's bright manner faded, and she looked ready to burst into tears. 'But it is such a lovely morning.' She glanced at Papa, obscured behind his newspaper, and said in a low voice, 'I need to walk, Fliss. Otherwise, I shall go positively mad.'

Surprised at her forcefulness but understanding from whence it stemmed, I readily agreed to go. I hated to see her becoming so strung up over Mr Pringle. *If a gentleman had to bear the same misery he inflicted on a woman with his silence, would he do it in quite so carefree a manner?* I wondered. Then again, we did not know the reason for Mr Pringle being quiet. Perhaps he had been called away on business with only a moment's notice to prepare for his journey. Furthermore, he may have had a carriage accident and be now lying in a hospital with broken bones, unable to send word or worse. It was not unheard-of for such a thing to have happened. Aunt's husband had died in just such a manner when his horse bolted and the carriage overturned.

So while I did not mention this to Harriet, it must've been on her mind, hence her imploring us to go for a long distracting walk.

After breakfast, I sought out my sturdiest boots and readied myself for our excursion. Papa urged us to take his umbrella for 'It may rain excessively, girls!' But it was a cumbersome, heavy thing; and I, for one, didn't want to carry it in the off chance of more than a light shower. Neither did Harriet as she replied, 'We will shelter under a tree, Papa. Do not worry.' Impatient to be away, she gave him a quick kiss on the cheek and strode outside, with me tailing after her.

Fifteen minutes later, we were on the outskirts of Steventon and walking along the main road to Overton. Having had to jump into the ditch to narrowly avoid two carriages, we were now at a stile and contemplating going cross-country.

'It is a more scenic route and faster certainly,' I said, putting up a hand to shade my eyes against the sun. 'But it goes right past Ashbury Manor.'

'Does it?' said Harriet innocently.

'You know very well it does. Is this your motive for dragging me out on a two-hour walk—to spy on Mr Pringle?'

'Of course not!' said Harriet, sounding suitably horrified.

'I would never suggest such a thing.' She lifted her skirt and proceeded to clamber over the stile. 'Though if we did happen to run into one of his servants, it would be only polite to ask about his health.'

'Hmm,' I muttered, not really wanting to be anywhere in the vicinity of Mr Stonyface if I could help it. But Harriet, it seemed, was determined to seek answers to Mr Pringle's whereabouts.

The path took us on a pleasant amble across green fields and several more stiles. Despite a small blister rubbing on my heel, I was enjoying being out of doors, breathing the fresh morning air and watching the swallows swoop in the clear blue sky. It was indeed a glorious day. Not the slightest hint of bad weather.

Before too long, we could sight the chimneys of Ashbury Manor in the distance. Edged by trees, the path wound around the back of the grand house, which, although we peered through the trees for a number of minutes to determine any movement, showed no signs of life.

'We could always knock on the servants' door for a cup of water,' suggested Harriet. Her forehead was bathed in light sweat from our exertions, and her expression was one of consternation.

'I think not, dearest,' I replied gently. There was a good chance of bumping into Mr Fitzroy the longer we lingered, and I didn't have a ready excuse for why we were snooping around. He wasn't a fool either, I'd give him that. No, much better to be on our way.

I looped my arm through Harriet's and tugged her along the path.

'I know it's difficult to wait, but I'm sure Mr Pringle has a reason for his absence. You will just have to be patient. It is a good test of character.'

'Oh, but I enjoyed his company so much!' she blurted.

'It was just two dances,' I reasoned. 'You shouldn't hang any hope of marrying him upon that.'

"Tis true,' she said gloomily. 'And it's not like I have any great fortune to entice him.'

'If Mr Pringle is a man of worth, he won't care about that.'

I sounded confident to my own ears, but inside, I sorely doubted that Harriet's looks and personality were enough to secure a man of his stature. Our position was in fact somewhat precarious. If anything happened to Papa, our house was entailed to go to our cousin and heir, one Mr Percival Humbleton. We'd met him once; he was the son of Mama's sister, a little older than us and now, by all accounts, a respected clergyman in Hertfordshire. But despite being our cousin and a man of God, he still had the power to turn us out of our home if he decided to sell it.

Aunt said she'd heard of such things happening, and the stories were truly distressing, hence why she was so eager for us to make good matches. But I preferred to stick my head in the sand and not dwell on it.

By the time we reached Overton, I was hot, parched, and perspiring like the proverbial piglet I'd been accused of resembling. Leaning against a pillar outside the haberdasher's, I urged Harriet to go in without me and said I'd join her presently when I'd collected myself. Blotting my forehead and upper lip with my lavender-scented handkerchief, I took in the various sights of the main street.

Overton, being a larger town than Steventon, was much busier, dirtier, and noisier. Carriages swung by, and horses' hooves kicked up clouds of dust. Small children squealed as mothers tugged them out of the way before they got mowed down. Clerks hurried past, carrying leather satchels bulging with papers, and then there were the crowds of general passers-by stopping to converse loudly with friends.

Through all this mayhem, I spied the face of someone that I wished to avoid at all costs. My heart started galloping in my chest as Mr Stonyface came striding down the street towards me. He was far enough away that he was still quite unaware of my presence as I was half hidden behind the pillar. I eyed the shop door; if I were hasty, I could sneak inside without an awkward encounter. But to do so, I should have to reveal my position. Perhaps he would stroll right past without me needing to acknowledge his presence. I didn't want to snub the man, but I was willing to feign ignorance and get away with it if I could.

Carefully, I opened my handkerchief and used it to shield my face, thus further obscuring me from his view. The pretence, I believed, was entirely successful until I heard a deep male voice intone dryly, 'Good day, Miss Blackburn.'

I lowered my handkerchief to find the gentleman himself gazing directly at me with a brooding expression. My throat contracted. 'Oh, g-good day, Mr Fitzroy,' I stuttered.

He touched his hat briefly and made as if to continue on but then paused and said, 'Are you in town for business?'

I was surprised that he seemed to want to converse. Perhaps he deemed it only polite.

'A business of sorts. My sister, Harriet, is purchasing ribbons.' I gestured towards the haberdasher's.

He lifted an eyebrow. 'Ah.'

Although I didn't wish to prolong the conversation, it now occurred to me I could press him for information to put Harriet's mind at ease.

'I trust you have settled into Ashbury Manor?' I asked.

Mr Fitzroy made a grunting noise, which I took to be assent. 'As well as can be expected.'

'Are the rooms not to your taste?' I asked, deadpan.

He stared at me suspiciously, unsure if I was teasing him. *Oh I was!*

'They are adequate,' he replied after duly considering my straight face to convince himself that I was serious. 'But the rooms, though spacious, have rather low ceilings. Being tall, one does tend to feel constricted in such surroundings.'

I nodded in feigned sympathy while thinking of my own house with its decidedly unspacious rooms and low ceilings. Oh dear, he'd positively hate it. But I needed to get him off the topic of houses.

'Is Mr Pringle, by any chance'—I looked beyond his broad shoulder down the street—'with you?'

'Unfortunately not. He had to go to London for an urgent family matter. I decided to take the spare carriage to town. But now that I'm here, I find that there is nothing particularly charming to look at.' His nose wrinkled, and I instantly took offence. It appeared he was including *me* in the uncharming sights of Overton. Oh, his manner was so disagreeable!

'I see,' I said coldly, and he shot me a glance.

'Present company excepted, of course,' he murmured and bowed, which I returned, my ruffled feathers somewhat smoothed. However, I didn't believe him in the slightest—it was all poppycock. I had heard well enough what he thought of me. But no matter!

40

'Will Mr Pringle be returning soon?' I asked innocently, determined to get the information I needed.

'I expect to see him tomorrow evening,' he replied. 'Depending on the roads. It looks like we're in for a spot of rain.' I glanced at the sky along with him and saw a large black cloud, born from the humidity, heading this way.

I nodded in agreement but, not wanting to get into a yawn-inducing discussion about the weather, edged towards the door front. 'Please excuse me. I should go and assist Harriet.'

'By all means. Don't let me keep you. Ribbons are, of course, most important.' A small smile appeared on his well-formed lips as if he were amused by his statement, and I couldn't help staring. Why, he looked actually human when he smiled. But at the same time, I found myself wanting to kick him in the shin for making fun at my expense. My feelings towards him were most disconcerting.

Before I could utter anything else, he doffed his hat and strode off back the way he'd come, no doubt to locate his carriage and get home before it rained. Bother, maybe I should have lugged Papa's umbrella to town after all. With another glance at the sky, I hurried into the haberdasher's, eager to soothe Harriet's angst now that I'd discovered Mr Pringle's return was imminent.

To say that Harriet was overjoyed at the news I imparted

was an understatement. She gripped the glove display table tightly with one hand while the other fluttered to her throat.

'Well!' she exclaimed. 'It was worth coming to town to hear that! Tomorrow night, you say? And an urgent family matter? I hope all is quite well.'

I absently stroked a pair of white silk gloves, the colour of which matched Mr Fitzroy's necktie perfectly. As I'd been standing on the shopfront, I'd been taller than usual and directly in front of his cravat. I'd seen it bob a bit as he'd swallowed before speaking.

'Fliss?' Harriet was looking at me, and I roused myself.

'All must be well if Mr Pringle is coming back. Otherwise, he'd stay in London,' I replied. 'Have you chosen your ribbons? It may rain, so we need to make haste.'

Harriet dutifully completed her purchase, and we began walking home. But no sooner had we reached the outskirts of Overton than the first fat drops started falling. With so much of our journey still to be undertaken, I feared we would be wet through within five minutes. I tugged on Harriet's arm to slow her. 'Perhaps we should shelter in town and wait for it to pass?'

She readily agreed, and we turned around. But a carriage was headed at a fast clip towards us, so we stood back from the road to let it pass. To my surprise, the driver slowed the horse as it drew near, and the window lowered. Mr Fitzroy's face appeared, and we all bowed accordingly.

'Excuse me, ladies, but I couldn't help but notice you're about to get drenched. Can I offer you a ride to Steventon?'

I hesitated, weighing the options: being stuck in a carriage with Mr Fitzroy for the next twenty minutes or walking over fields with a sodden dress. It was a difficult decision. But before I could reply, a crack of thunder sounded in the distance; and Harriet jumped and said hastily, 'Thank you, sir! We'd be much obliged!'

The carriage door swung open, and a large elegant hand with neatly manicured nails extended, which she took; then she hopped up inside. There was nothing I could do but follow suit, but I declined his hand, being able to fend for myself. Although he'd called it "the spare", the carriage was still finely upholstered and much grander than our old buggy. However, it did feel rather small with Mr Fitzroy's large frame taking up most of the space. I had to take particular care that my knees did not knock against his. He rapped on the red-silk-lined roof, and we set off.

Harriet attempted to make polite small talk, to which Mr Fitzroy gave curt one-word replies. But I was content to watch the rain now falling in sheets across the green fields from a slate-coloured sky.

'Do you walk often to Overton, Miss Blackburn?' he

asked suddenly, directing the question to me.

'Not if I can help it,' I said. 'I prefer to ride George, though he needs some convincing if the distance is over a mile.'

'George is our buggy horse,' supplied Harriet helpfully. 'He's a stubborn brute. Only Fliss can manage him.'

I smiled at that. 'Yes, he's a man that certainly needs a firm hand, but I'm up to the task.'

One of Mr Fitzroy's eyebrows quirked, and I flushed a little when I realised what I'd said. 'Er, I mean, he usually toes the line if you give him some extra oats in the morning before setting off.'

'Extra oats indeed,' replied Mr Fitzroy with a smirk. 'I know I'm always more amenable with a full stomach.'

It was on the tip of my tongue to enquire exactly how much more amenable when, fortunately, there was a 'Whoa, boy!' from outside. My remark could have been construed as flirtatious, and the last thing I wanted to do was flirt with Mr Fitzroy.

The carriage slowed considerably, and the gentleman lowered the window and stuck his head out to see what the issue was.

'Just a couple taking up too much of the road,' he said, wiping the rain off his face with a handkerchief. 'They didn't hear the carriage.'

As we passed the 'couple', I caught a glimpse of who they were: Samuel and a young woman. He was holding his jacket over her head; and as she tilted her smiling face up towards him, he took the opportunity, at that very moment, to lean down and place a kiss upon her pouty lips!

I drew a shocked breath, not believing what my eyes had seen. Samuel had professed his interest in *me*; and yet here he was, in broad daylight, carrying on with a floozy. My face grew hot as humiliation burned and tears pricked my eyes. Harriet had seen the display as well but could do nothing to comfort me being seated directly opposite.

'Maybe we could speed up a little now,' she murmured worriedly, seeing my pained expression.

Mr Fitzroy was looking at me curiously. 'Are you quite well, Miss Blackburn?'

I nodded my head mutely as embarrassment turned to rage. *How could Samuel do this to me? The two-timing lout!*

I had permitted him to be amorous with me because I liked him despite his lack of fortune and he was the handsomest man in the village. But it appeared that Mr Green's attention was now wholly given to another. And I was a fool for believing the words of affection he'd whispered to me in a dark hay barn.

Chapter 4

Suddenly, I found it difficult to breathe in the constricted space of the carriage. The wide open fields looked much more inviting, even in the pouring rain. I scrabbled at the latch, intending to make a leap for it, but Mr Fitzroy's warm firm hand closed around mine.

'What are you doing?' His tone was one of concern, but I didn't trust that he really was worried. He'd made his feelings and opinion of me quite clear.

I shook off his hand. 'How dare you touch me! Let me out of this carriage. *At once.*'

'No,' he said calmly, holding on to the latch so I couldn't release the door. 'I shan't. You are being irrational, and in that state, you are liable to do yourself an injury.'

'Irrational? I'm not irrational. I'm perfectly in my right mind, and I demand you open this door!' I cried.

'No. I. Shan't,' he repeated slowly and clearly as if he were talking to an imbecile, which made my blood boil.

'Fliss, please,' Harriet begged. 'We're almost home.'

My sister's distress cut through my ire and touched the saner part of my brain. So I sat with my eyes closed, breathing hard, keeping the cascading hurt and anger locked tight inside me. Mr Fitzroy did not speak again during this time; if he'd said anything remotely provoking, I would not have been responsible for my actions!

As soon as the carriage halted outside our house, I threw open the door and made to alight. But in my haste, I stumbled, my hand clutching wildly at the air until a strong grip around my waist steadied me.

'Here.' Mr Fitzroy guided my foot onto the small step. 'Careful, it's slippery.' His hand moved from my waist when I was anchored and took mine to guide me down. When I let go of his hand, out of the corner of my eye, I saw him open and close it rapidly as if in pain. But I had hardly touched him, let alone strained his fingers!

I heard Harriet thanking Mr Fitzroy for the ride home, but I couldn't look at him as I was now feeling ashamed about my outburst. I managed a half-hearted bow and scurried up the path and into the house.

I went straight to my room and burrowed into my eiderdown, creating a kind of cocoon for my misery. Strangely, I was so distraught that I could not even summon tears. The ones that had brimmed in the carriage had been chased away by anger, and I shook with vexation and even moaned a little in my darkened lair. There was no way that

I could marry Samuel now, even if I had been dragging my heels about doing so. If he turned around and asked me tomorrow, I'd have to refuse him. There was no way on earth I could be married to a man who I had seen bestowing affection on another woman—in a country lane no less!

It seemed like half an hour that I suffered, but it was probably only a few minutes later that Harriet was there and cradling my prone patchwork quilted form. 'Oh, Fliss. Trust it to have been Samuel of all people! How utterly mortifying for you.'

I let out a loud groan of despair, and she rubbed my back and made soothing noises. 'I know, dearest, I know. He's wounded you deeply.'

I sat up and flung the cover back, impatiently swiping strands of hair from my sweaty face. 'Even worse is that Mr Fitzroy witnessed the slight! He saw me dancing with Samuel and making eyes at him. Now to have him learn of him discarding me in this manner—I shall die of shame!'

Harriet rubbed my arm sympathetically. 'Dearest, I do not think Mr Fitzroy even knew it was Samuel on the road or saw what he did. I am quite sure that he was facing away from the window when it occurred. Besides, he seemed more concerned that you would fling yourself out of the carriage and do yourself an injury.'

Her lips twitched, and I frowned. 'Oh, I see. Now you're

making fun of me.'

'Of course not! But you are a little more concerned with Mr Fitzroy's opinion of you than the loss of Samuel, don't you think?'

I sighed and lay back on the pillow and pressed my hand around my chest area, trying to discern the current level of pain.

'It is true that the heartache has lessened even during the short time we have been speaking,' I admitted. 'But I shan't ever forgive Samuel for making a fool of me.'

. Harriet shook her head emphatically. 'I never much liked him anyway. You can do much better than Mr Green. But if you do meet someone else, just please promise me you won't go sneaking out at night. It's unseemly.'

'Yes, I promise,' I said idly, not really believing I should keep such a promise if my passions were duly stirred. Indeed, now that I was thinking clearly, it was plain that Samuel was not right for me. There were a number of things about him that irritated me intensely, such as making loud chewing noises when he ate and talking endlessly about crop rotations, farm animals, and market prices—if we were married these things would become even more irritating.

Then there was the small matter of my being terrified to have children after what had happened to my mother. It was the thing that I had wanted to discuss with Samuel after the dance as I thought he should be aware of it before he made me a serious offer. Being from a large family, I knew that he would likely expect me to produce a number of strapping sons to carry on the Green lineage. Thankfully, I'd never let our amorous encounters stray into that intimate a nature, or I might have had to marry him by default. I wasn't sure exactly what he might have said to alleviate my nagging fear, but that was now a conversation we would never have. He'd made his own haystack, and now he had to lie in it. No, as of this moment, I was completely unattached to Samuel Green forever more; and I was free to spend time with any other gentleman I liked. It was a pity, however, that there was no other gentleman that I was remotely attracted to.

* * *

Our excursion into town had another unfortunate consequence: Harriet caught a cold. It was severe enough to make her feel extremely poorly and unable to leave her bed for almost a week. It was no trouble on my part to play nursemaid as she was a most uncomplaining patient and bore her symptoms (a headache, runny nose, and an irritating cough) without complaint, indeed as well as she had borne Mr Pringle's silence. I thought that I should be struck down too because of my extreme emotional shock about Samuel—but no, I was as hale and hearty as ever and had no ill effects from it. To be quite sure, whenever our cook, Sue, made Harriet horehound tea with honey, I also drank a cup. And when she prepared her a herbal steam inhalation, I requested another bowl for myself to keep her company. To be *extra sure* of my health, I also gargled some vinegar from the pantry (but only once because it tasted horrid!).

Taking heart in Mr Fitzroy's information about Mr Pringle's return and despite feeling under the weather, Harriet could not hide her anticipation every time the post came. I tried to keep her emotions balanced on the matter, but unfortunately, when one is ill and letters do not appear when one wants them to, it can send one's spirits into a slump. I could not magically make a letter from Mr Pringle appear short of pretending to write it myself! All I could do was distract her from dwelling upon it with cheerful discourse. Aunt Snelling also dropped by several times with the latest village gossip, an abundance of lemons from her tree, and a mewling kitten she'd rescued from three youths who had been teasing it, which provided much welcome diversion.

Still, it was with some relief that I excused myself from nurse duty one afternoon and left Harriet, much improved and sitting up in bed reading her Gothic novel, to visit Jane. I found her in the sty, emptying a bucket of slops to a litter of hungry piglets. 'Hello, little sisters,' I said, peering over the slatted fence. 'My, you are greedy wee things but so much prettier than us!'

Jane chortled. 'I fear Mr Fitzroy will never live that remark down for as long as you live, Fliss.'

'Longer,' I replied. 'I will come back from the grave and haunt him. He'll awaken in the middle of the night to ghostly oinking and think he's gone mad.'

We left the noisy piggies to their meal and made our way up the slate path. 'Henry is entertaining a friend, and Father is tutoring his students, so it's a rather male-dominated house this afternoon. But we shan't be disturbed upstairs.'

Pausing at the kitchen to request tea and cake, we ran upstairs to her parlour and I made myself comfortable on the sofa.

'Is that another letter to Cassie?' I asked, seeing numerous inked pages spread out to dry on the table. I inclined my head to see, but she tucked them out of sight into her writing slope before I could get a good look.

'Yes, nosy one.'

'You always write so much to her. Honestly, if Harriet

were to go away, I doubt I'd be able to summon the energy to scribble a postcard.'

'How is Harriet? I heard she was unwell.'

My eyebrows raised slightly. Aunt, I assumed, was the instigator of that information. News travelled quickly in our small village. I wondered if Harriet's cold had reached Mr Pringle's ears yet and if it might encourage him to pen a supportive epistle.

'Coming right, I expect her to be up and about in the next day or so. She's past the worst of it. Now she's just bored.'

'How did it occur?' Jane unlaced her boots and joined me on the sofa, tucking her stockinged feet under her. 'Not from the dance surely. That was a while ago.'

'No, we walked to Overton last week and got caught in a shower coming back. Luckily, Mr Fitzroy came by and offered us a ride in his carriage at just the right moment, or she could have been a lot worse.'

'Did he now? Well, I hadn't heard that part of it. Do let me hear the whole story!' Jane's eyes burned with curiosity, and I knew she wouldn't tell anyone apart from Cassandra, who was discretion itself. So I relayed how I had been trying to hide from him outside the haberdasher's.

'And how did he look? What was his manner?'

'As haughty as ever,' I said, sipping my tea and eyeing the generous chunk of moist ginger cake we'd been given. I sunk the knife into it and took a generous helping for my plate. After eating invalid food on Harriet's behalf all week, I was starving. 'He was polite enough to stop and converse, I suppose. But I had no wish to prolong the conversation.'

'Of course not.' Jane nodded her agreement.

'I talked with him only to find out Mr Pringle's whereabouts, and he supplied that readily.'

'Yes, he'd been to London.'

'Oh, you knew?'

'I found out yesterday from Father. He mentioned Mr Pringle had returned.'

The strong ginger from the cake and Jane's confirmation mingled to make my spirits feel quite uplifted for Harriet's sake. *Thank goodness*, I thought in relief. *No more surmising. He's truly back!*

'But carry on,' said Jane impatiently, waving her cake fork at me. 'Get to the part with the carriage.'

'Well, when we were walking back, it started raining. And Mr Fitzroy was passing and enquired if we would like a ride. Harriet said yes before I could stop her. If I were by myself, I would have preferred getting wet. It was most awkward sitting in the carriage with him. He's not the easiest person to converse with.'

I paused, feeling reluctant to impart what happened next, and took a deep breath.

'Unfortunately, we happened to pass by Samuel and a young woman. They were ...' I shook my head but could not say the word. *Kissing.*

'Samuel is engaged, Flissy,' said Jane gently. 'I found that out yesterday as well. When Father walks into town to visit people, he finds out all kinds of news. I'm so sorry.'

I lowered my plate to my lap, the ginger cake suddenly losing its appeal. I stared at her.

'*Engaged*? Are you sure?'

'Yes, Samuel asked Father if he could marry them in three months' time.'

I swallowed, and she grasped my hand.

'I knew that he was lost to me when I saw them together, but hearing the words aloud makes it sound so final. Who is she?'

'Penelope Matlock, a farmer's daughter from Overton. She and Samuel became acquainted a month ago at the assembly that was held there. Both sets of parents were approving of the match, and he was encouraged to propose. However, apparently, it took a stern word from his father for him to follow through.'

I shifted uncomfortably. 'I assume that was because he

still had some lingering regard for me.'

No wonder Samuel had been bringing up the subject of marriage more insistently lately; he had another woman waiting in the wings! Anger rose in me again, but as quickly as it came, it was dispelled. I must be a very accepting kind of person to forgive him for this slight. A less benign type of woman wouldn't be so understanding. At this rate, I'd be congratulating him *and* attending the wedding without so much as a snub!

'You must be awfully cut up about it,' said Jane sympathetically. 'After all, he was always banging on about asking *you* to marry him.'

'It has taken me by surprise, but I now think it a blessing rather than a curse.' I told her about Samuel's propensity to chew loudly and talk about crop rotations.

Jane giggled. 'Oh dear. I suppose Miss Matlock will find out his annoying habits in due course. You know what they say: "marry in haste, repent at leisure".'

I didn't smile, and Jane looked at me.

'Don't be glum, Fliss. There is a better match for you, I know it. Someone much more worthy than Samuel Green.'

I sniffed. 'To be quite honest, I have no interest in anyone. I'm off men entirely.'

Jane smiled mischievously. 'What about Mr Fitzroy?'

I looked at her, slightly shocked. '*Him?* There isn't a man on earth I'd rather *not* marry. Imagine waking up every morning to see those piercing eyes boring into you and that grumpy expression.' I shuddered at the thought. 'Besides, he has a twitch.'

'A twitch?'

'Yes, in his right hand. When he transferred me out of the carriage, he opened and closed it several times as if he were in pain. It was most odd.'

'That is strange,' said Jane thoughtfully. 'Maybe he has some kind of nervous condition? I'll look it up later in Father's medical book.'

I yawned and stretched. 'Anyway, enough of Mr Stonyface. I should go and tend to the invalid and see if she wants to take a small stroll in the garden. Don't get up. I'll see myself out,' I said, levering myself off the sofa. 'Thank you for the tea, and please give my compliments to your cook for the ginger cake. It was most ... stringent.'

'All right. Tell Harriet I shall come and visit you both in a few days. Let us hope that she receives her longed-for letter in the meantime.'

'We can only pray,' I said, not feeling too confident of it occurring.

At the doorway, I looked back to see Jane was busily writing at her desk.

Speaking of letters, she is probably finishing hers to Cassie now that she has information to impart about my failed romance, I thought. In some way, I wished I was Cassie receiving the news as told through Jane's sharp-witted observations rather than being the subject of it. But at the same time, I didn't want to censor her as I knew writing gave her great pleasure and that she would always refer to me in the most sympathetic terms.

PART TWO

An Unexpected Guest

Chapter 5

The next day, Harriet was well enough to get dressed and come downstairs to partake in breakfast. She still looked a little peaky, but Sue made her a soft-boiled egg and some buttered toast, which she consumed readily enough. We were lingering over a second cup of tea and discussing our plans for the day when Mary appeared with a letter for Papa.

'Thank you, Mary,' he said and laid it on the table. As he was reading his paper, he showed no immediate inclination to open it. Harriet cleared her throat softly, and I looked over, thinking she was ridding herself of some phlegm. But she was quite rigid, holding her cup of tea aloft but not drinking out of it. She widened her eyes at me and then swivelled them to the letter, which had a fancy red wax seal on it. Oh! I could tell what she was thinking—that it was from Mr Pringle and that she needed Papa to open it and tell us its contents right away. Her eyebrows moved up and down in consternation. She was right—he could be another twenty minutes at his paper! There was nothing for it.

'Papa, may I ask who the letter is from?' I said boldly, taking the reins. 'It looks important.'

He lowered his paper. 'I do not know. I haven't opened it. I shall do so in a minute.'

'Might you be persuaded to open it more quickly than a minute?' Papa glanced at me and then at Harriet, who was trying but failing to keep her composure.

'Very well. Since you two are suddenly so interested in my affairs.'

He broke the seal, opened the flaps, and perused the letter, which appeared to be quite short.

'It is from Mr Pringle,' he said, sounding pleased. 'A most cordial invitation to dine with him and Mr Fitzroy at Ashbury Manor five nights hence.'

'Just you, Papa, or ...?' I asked.

'No, he's invited all of us, along with the Austens.'

Harriet emitted a long, slow breath. 'That is wonderful news!' she said.

'Are you sure you will feel up to it, Harriet?' enquired Papa. 'You may like to stay here ...'

Harriet shook her head sharply, her cheeks now showing a faint flush of colour. 'I am nearly well now, Papa. And in five days, I shall be fully returned to health.'

I quelled a smile. Even if Harriet were on death's door, she'd insist on attending.

Papa nodded and, upon my asking, handed over the letter. I scanned it eagerly to ascertain any hidden meaning that would comfort Harriet further. But apart from it being penned by an elegant hand and in a hospitable manner, there was nothing.

I passed it along to her, saying, 'It's a good letter.'

'It *is* a good letter,' she agreed, running a finger over the swirling ink as if she might surmise Mr Pringle's true intentions for the invitation. I too wasn't sure of what he intended with his supper party. Was it because he wished to see Harriet again or simply wanted to forge deeper connections with the families of Steventon—one of which provided him with excellent hogget and the other which could make his suits?

While I pondered upon this and the unwelcome realisation that I would be forced into Mr Fitzroy's company once more, Mary appeared again at the doorway.

'Excuse me, sir, there's another letter for you.'

'Goodness, I am popular this morning,' said Papa, beckoning her in and taking it from her hand. 'Thank you, Mary.' She curtsied and left the room.

This second letter was smaller than the first and had a simple wafer seal rather than a wax one. As Mr Pringle's supper was firmly established and I could breathe a sigh of relief on Harriet's part, I wasn't too concerned about the other letter. But seeing Papa frown when reading it made me curious.

'Who is it from?' I asked him.

'Mr Humbleton, your cousin. He's inviting himself to stay with us for a couple of weeks. And the day he arrives falls exactly before when we are to dine at Ashbury.'

My heart sank. The one time I had met him I had found him very dull company indeed. But as the heir to our home, we couldn't exactly say 'No, don't come'. So we would have to bear his presence as best we could, and I fervently hoped he had improved with age.

'Does he say why he's coming?'

'Not in so many words. In fact, it's all quite vague. Have a look and see if you girls can determine his intention.'

I took the letter and laid it on the table so Harriet could peruse it also. It was a short, almost perfunctory, note to say that he was taking leave from his clerical duties for a fortnight and desired to visit his Steventon relations. He would be arriving four days hence in the afternoon, around three o'clock, he thought, and would we be so kind as to prepare him a bed and that he looked forward to reacquainting himself with his fair cousins. I assumed that to mean Harriet and myself.

'It *seems* innocent enough,' I said after a pause. 'Though a little presumptuous. Surely, he knows we have only three bedrooms. That means Harriet and I will have to share, unless we put him in the storage cupboard.'

Harriet tittered.

'I know it is a disruption, but we shall have to make do,' replied Papa evenly. 'I'll write to Mr Pringle and say there will be two more to attend his supper party.'

'Pray, why two?' asked Harriet.

'Because I shall tell him Mr Humbleton is visiting, and Mrs Snelling is required as your chaperone.'

Papa didn't expand on his reasoning, but I knew him well enough to surmise what he was thinking—that if he didn't invite Aunt, there was a strong likelihood of him being saddled with Mr Humbleton for the evening. He was relying on her talent for conversation (read: gossip) to keep him engaged. Very devious indeed!

* * *

My spirits leading up to the supper party were quite in contrast to my sister's. Harriet's were high because she was assured of seeing Mr Pringle again. Mine were subdued because I had to relinquish my bedroom to our guest as well as move my dresses to Harriet's wardrobe, where they were squashed in next to hers. I also had to clear out my dresser drawers and my bookshelf. I wasn't sure what Mr

Humbleton's reading tastes were, but I didn't want him perusing my romantic novels! It was all a big upheaval and one that I couldn't help grumbling about to Harriet. What was so important that he needed to visit us? And two weeks was a rather large amount of time for him to stay. But it seemed we didn't have a choice in the matter. So we were forced to squeeze in together until he left.

As good as his word, Mr Humbleton arrived promptly at three o'clock the day before we were to dine at Ashbury. It was almost as if he had planned it to be so, but I doubted our clergyman cousin had mystical powers for seeing into the future. He'd simply turned up at an inconvenient time and would now have to accompany us. Aunt had also accepted the invitation and was looking forward to the occasion immensely. I wasn't as enthusiastic, but I supposed the increase in number meant there was less chance of me having to talk to Mr Stonyface. I was still feeling embarrassed about my outburst in the carriage and knew I needed to apologise to him, but I had a feeling if the occasion arose to do so, the words might stick in my throat.

After the introductions were completed, Papa asked Mr Humbleton if he would like to rest after his journey or take tea in the parlour.

'Some refreshment would be most welcome, thank you,'

our cousin replied, bowing again.

'Excellent. I'll have your bag taken to your room.' Papa gestured to Mary, who had been hovering in the background, and she quickly acquiesced. 'If you need anything while you are here, just ring for Mary, and she will see to it. She is most amenable.'

The two men walked down the hallway conversing, and Harriet and I followed behind. So far, Mr Humbleton had seemed genial, and his looks had certainly improved in the last six years since I had met him at my aunt and uncle's house in Hertfordshire. I remembered a tall, gangly youth with a slouch and not much else to commend him. He still had the height, along with a full head of copper-toned brown hair and a face that was pleasant rather than handsome to look at. But he'd filled out and stood straighter; and his eyes darted about, looking at items—the vase on the table, the pictures on the wall, the rug—as if noting the details of his surroundings for future contemplation. Harriet and I had both been given this inspection also. *Had we passed muster?* I wondered.

When we were seated on adjacent sofas, Mr Humbleton ran his fingers over a cushion cover Harriet had painstakingly embroidered with the phrase 'Love and Be Loved', and he murmured, 'Fine work.'

He certainly seemed to be interested in soft furnishings.

'I do hope you find everything to your taste,' said Papa politely. 'I'm sure you are used to much finer parlours.'

Mr Humbleton met his gaze steadily. 'Indeed I am not. I was just this moment thinking to myself what an excellent aspect this room has. It catches the afternoon sunlight perfectly. If I were an artist, I would most certainly feel the urge to take to my easel and paint. Sadly, I am not blessed with such talents.'

Not being able to help myself, I enquired, 'Where do your talents lie, Mr Humbleton? Are they perhaps more of an ecclesiastical nature?'

He smiled at me affably. 'Indeed, Miss Felicity. I like to think I do justice to my calling. As well as the Sunday sermon, I provide counsel to my parish whenever it is required and have been told I do much to ease their spiritual suffering.'

'Do you like to read at all, cousin?' This from Harriet, who always had her nose stuck in a book.

'Only the Bible' came the reply. 'Anything else, I fear, is much too diverting from the one true path.'

No one quite knew what to say to this, but I was glad that I'd removed my romantic novels to Harriet's room.

The ensuing conversation with Mr Humbleton, unfortunately, did not elevate much beyond the weather, confirming my previously formed opinion of him. After his tea was drunk and a slice of pound cake was eaten and declared 'very palatable', he retired upstairs to rest and read the Bible before supper, leaving us still unclear as to the purpose of his visit.

***

On the evening of the supper party, we rode in Mr Humbleton's carriage to Ashbury Manor. He'd taken one look at our buggy and deemed it unsuitable for such a venture. Aunt rode with us also; and with five persons (not to mention our dresses, shawls, top hats, and walking sticks jammed in together), it was hot and stifling. I was relieved when we arrived.

Mr Humbleton handed Harriet down from the carriage and then myself.

Before letting go of my gloved hand, he pressed it slightly and murmured, 'I look forward to becoming better acquainted with you, Miss Felicity, beginning this evening.'

A trickle of unease ran down my spine. For politeness' sake, I could do nothing but nod and follow Harriet up the steps. But I now had a strong suspicion as to why Mr Humbleton was visiting. The meaning of him wishing to become 'better acquainted' with me could not be misconstrued: he was looking for a wife! The notion filled me with dread. I liked him even less than Mr Stonyface, and that was saying something! This evening would be trying indeed if I now had to avoid two gentlemen. Thankfully, Jane would be there. And maybe if she liked the look of him, I could steer Mr Humbleton in her direction!

So intent was I on dissecting this piece of information and formulating my plan of action that I almost bumped into Harriet in the entranceway.

'Is it not wonderful, Fliss?' she whispered, gazing up at the high coffered ceiling. A wide staircase wound up to the first floor, which was adorned with archways and lit here and there with small lamps.

'Indeed,' I whispered back. 'But remember, it is only rented. He does not own it.'

'But still, he has the means to rent it. That is something.'

A footman took our shawls, and I was wondering what we were to do next when a Welsh accent rang out, 'Good evening!' Mr Pringle came striding across the black-and-white-tiled floor with a welcoming smile on his face. He cut a fine figure in a fashionable dark-blue tailcoat, brocade waistcoat, high-collared shirt and white linen cravat, along with a pair of well-fitting breeches. I felt Harriet sway a little—whether it was because of his tight breeches or simply seeing him in the flesh after all this time, I was not sure, but I gripped her elbow for support nonetheless!

'Miss Blackburn.' He bowed to Harriet.

She dipped slightly, inclining her head towards him. 'Mr Pringle.' I rejoiced that her voice was firm and clear and did not shake at all to belie her inner feelings, which I was sure were all aflutter.

'Miss Blackburn.' It was my turn to bow.

'And Mr Blackburn and Mrs Snelling. How delightful! I trust your journey here was pleasant?'

'Oh, yes,' said Aunt. 'We came in a carriage rather than the buggy, you see. So it was quite comfortable.'

'Wonderful!'

There was a shuffle as my cousin, who had decided it was time to make his presence known, stepped forward.

'Mr Percival Humbleton at your service, cousin to the Misses Blackburn.'

He bowed so low that I heard his neck creak. When he was again upright, the prattle started. 'I must say, Mr Pringle, your home is most impressive. Such fine stair banisters!'

Mr Pringle didn't falter. 'Thank you, sir. You are most kind and very welcome. Now let us join the rest of our party in the parlour while we wait for supper to be served.'

We moved off after him down the hallway, and I steeled myself to see Mr Fitzroy. But upon entering, I found that there was Jane, her brother Henry, and Mr and Mrs Austen.

There was no sign of Mr Pringle's stern friend. Perhaps he had decided not to attend? Having prepared for this moment for several nerve-racking days, it was a disconcerting to find I needn't have bothered.

I accepted a glass of Madeira wine from the footman and sipped it, then took a couple of larger swigs. The warming effect of the liquor made me feel more relaxed, and I looked around the room, admiring the general splendour.

My gaze alighted on Jane, who was wearing a fetching blue silk gown with a delicate white embroidered neckline. She was observing Mr Humbleton conversing with Papa, Mr Austen, and Mr Pringle from across the room with a critical eye; and I wondered what she would make of him. I sidled over.

'Our cousin Mr Percival Humbleton, in case you were wondering,' I said in a low voice.

'Ah, that will be the reason for the extra place at the table. Is he visiting you for long?'

'Two weeks,' I replied, resisting the urge to wrinkle my nose. 'Would you like me to take you over to meet him?'

Jane glanced at me sharply. 'I can wait for Father to make the introductions.'

She wasn't a fool. My hope that I'd be able to divert Mr Humbleton's attention onto her sank like a stone. I was going to have to think of something (or someone) else fast. I took another large sip of wine to fortify myself.

'At least Mr Stonyface isn't here,' I said to her in a low voice. 'That would make this evening very unpleasant indeed.'

'But he is,' Jane returned, peering over my head. 'He's just come in. He's talking with Henry.'

Slowly, I turned and saw Mr Fitzroy, tall and stiff postured, dressed impeccably in evening black. My stomach clenched at seeing his handsome face, cool and austere. His eyes locked with mine, and a tangible shudder went through me. I sensed that he might come over, and then I'd have to go through with my apology speech. Quickly, I turned my back to him and drained my wine.

'Goodness, you must be thirsty,' said Jane. 'Let me get you another.'

Before I could stop her, she'd taken my empty glass and whisked away to the footman for a refill, leaving me vulnerable to the attentions of Mr Fitzroy. Alarmed, I looked over to Harriet, who was conversing happily with Papa, Aunt, and Mr Pringle. I needed to go over there now and join their posse ...

'Miss Felicity.' Mr Humbleton appeared by my side without warning. 'I have just been informed that supper is to be served forthwith. May I escort you into the dining room?'

I groaned inwardly. If he escorted me in, he would then be sitting next to me for the duration of the meal. 'Yes, you may,' I said dully, and he proffered his elbow. I took it, resigned to my fate—for the supper at least.

Chapter 6

I conceded that being Mr Humbleton's supper partner had its advantages. He talked about nothing of consequence and in such great quantity so as to not require an intelligent answer in return. This meant I was fully able to enjoy the excellent supper with a 'Mmmhmm' or 'You don't say?' inserted as a response.

The food was rich and plentiful, and the courses kept coming. After finishing the creamy pea soup, I availed myself of the baked stuffed pike and then a few slices of a most delicious roast haunch of venison with juniper berry sauce accompanied by various vegetables.

Mr Humbleton, I noticed, ate sparingly, taking only a little from each of the dishes. After he'd tasted a forkful from the modest dollop of mashed potato he'd placed on his plate, he cleared his throat to catch Mr Pringle's attention on his right-hand side. Mr Pringle was wholly absorbed in conversing with Harriet and didn't notice. Mr Humbleton coughed louder until, finally, Mr Pringle looked around, startled.

'Sir, I simply must commend you', began my cousin, 'on

the excellence of your mashed potatoes. Rarely have I encountered a vegetable as outstanding as this. Pray, from which field do they originate?'

Jane, on my other side, snuffled into her napkin; and oh no, I could feel a hysterical giggle welling. I mustn't, couldn't laugh! I pinched my nostrils, and my face went red with the effort of trying to keep it in. I happened to catch sight of Mr Fitzroy on the other side of the table, his eyes gleaming with amusement. If the question had been directed at him, his reply, I fear, may have been designed to prolong the spectacle.

Luckily, Mr Pringle had much better manners.

'Ah, thank you,' he said with no trace of guile. 'I believe they come from here in Steventon, but I would have to check with the cook. I can do so later if you would like?'

Mr Humbleton nodded, appeased, and proceeded to take tiny forkfuls of potato and sigh in ecstasy as if he had been visited by the Rapture. He was so ignorant of his affectations that it was decidedly entertaining! But it was one thing to find one's cousin amusing and quite another for him to be the subject of a man's sport. I suspected Mr Fitzroy was just such a man, and I did my best not to look directly at him for fear of encouraging him to say something—a difficult feat when his mere presence drew my attention unwillingly. I watched surreptitiously as those elegant large hands of his deftly cut up a slice of venison with no sign of a tremor. If he did indeed have a nervous complaint, he was hiding it well. He paused to drink from his glass of wine, and his eyes met mine. Hastily, I returned to my own meal, my face flushing and a tight, breathless feeling rising in my chest. I refused to think that Mr Fitzroy had caused this sensation; it was no doubt a symptom of eating too much!

I laid down my knife and fork on the side of the plate and noticed Jane ploughing through a giant dollop of mashed potato with as much enjoyment as Mr Humbleton. Hmm, another plan took shape in my mind. Jane's sister, Cassandra, could be the perfect diversion for his attention. She was more his age and would make an excellent clergyman's wife. The timing was crucial, however. She needed to arrive before he left.

'Jane, when is Cassie expected back?' I enquired of her.

'Next week,' she replied. 'Though her stay might be extended. They are having such excellent weather in Kent.'

This was frustrating news indeed. I could only pray for rain to drench southeast England to speed her hasty return and that I could throw Mr Humbleton off my scent meanwhile.

Supper concluded after a dessert of trifle and gooseberry tart (which no one could manage much of); and the men retired to smoke cigars, drink port, and whatever it was that men did behind closed doors. Finally, I was free of Mr Humbleton, and my shoulders and spirits lifted considerably. I tried not to think about what ridiculous things he was saying to Mr Pringle and Mr Fitzroy—and what they might think about him and, in turn, my family.

I focused my attention on Harriet instead. She, Jane, and I sat in the bay window, well away from Aunt and Mrs Austen, who were sharing village gossip on the sofa.

'Tell us, Harriet', said Jane, her voice brimming with curiosity, 'how did you fare with Mr Pringle? He seemed most attentive to you during supper.'

'Indeed, he was,' Harriet replied, arranging her skirts. 'I could not fault him for temperament nor manners. He was a most obliging host and insisted I had the choicest cut of venison.'

'Oof, that venison was marvellous, as was the entire supper,' I said, patting my stomach. 'If you were to marry him, you may end up not being able to fit through the doorway.'

'I am sure he does not eat like that daily, especially since he was so very delicious ...'

Jane and I looked at each other and giggled.

'I meant to say "it",' said Harriet, correcting herself hurriedly, her cheeks fiery. '"It" meaning "the supper" was so very delicious.'

'You can't take it back now, dearest,' I said with a smile. 'Your feelings about our gracious host have been made known and in his own house no less.'

Harriet let out a groan.

Jane patted her hand. 'Do not fret. At least it was only our trustworthy ears who heard the words.'

We glanced collectively over at Aunt and Mrs Austin, who were twittering away. If they knew Harriet thought Mr Pringle was 'very delicious', it would not take long for the information to reach the gentleman's own ears, and who knew how receptive he would be to such prattle before he had made his own feelings known. Harriet might find herself passed over for a slip of the tongue!

When the men returned to the parlour an hour later, smelling of cigar smoke and strong liquor, Mr Humbleton's countenance was animated. But Mr Fitzroy's face was even stonier than usual. It was most curious. I wondered what had been discussed to create such a mood. I supposed I would never know!

'Now could any of you young ladies be persuaded to entertain us on the pianoforte?' enquired Mr Pringle with an encouraging smile. 'I'm afraid it has been played only once by myself since we arrived and in a rather ham-fisted manner. But I do so enjoy a jolly tune.'

To my relief, Harriet said she would be delighted to perform, and I fervently hoped that I wouldn't be expected to play. Although we both had had lessons growing up, Harriet was the superior musician—mostly because she was more patient than I when it came to practising. I had much preferred to be outdoors or read a book than tinkle away on the ivory keys. As a result, my technique had suffered somewhat. I also suspected that I had a tin ear. No, Harriet could take up the mantle for the Blackburn sisters. I was content enough to enjoy the melody from the safety of the sofa.

After Harriet had finished her well-executed song, there was a round of applause, the loudest clapping emitting from Mr Pringle; and she smiled at him, blushed, and curtsied prettily. He did seem taken with her, if one could judge such things from enthusiastic clapping and calls of 'Brava!'

'Who's next?' he asked, looking round expectantly at me and Jane from his chair. 'Miss Austen, surely, you could oblige us with a tune? Your father told me you play very nicely.'

'Father, you didn't!' Jane scolded him.

Mr Austen inclined his head towards his daughter and smiled. 'I believe I did.'

Jane ducked her head. 'Well, I suppose I could manage a song if my audience was a sympathetic one.'

We assured her that indeed we would not judge her for a bum note or two. But when she started, it was instantly obvious to everyone that Jane's playing was decidedly on par and even, dare I say, superior to Harriet's. She gave us a most rousing rendition of 'The Irish Washerwoman', and the upbeat tempo had our feet tapping in time.

Of course we insisted upon an encore, and she dutifully played 'Over the Hills and Far Away', which was equally as lively and earned a solid round of applause.

'Jane, that was wonderful!' I exclaimed as she returned to the sofa. 'I didn't know you could play so well.'

'Neither did I,' she replied modestly. 'It is because I have been bored without Cassie and only have my writing to occupy me. Father has been encouraging me to play, so I've found myself practising for a couple of hours each day. I must have improved.'

'I'll say. Well done!' I said, feeling a bit envious of her talent. But I pushed it aside. She *had* practised, and I could hardly be jealous when I hadn't touched our pianoforte for years.

'Miss Felicity, I believe it is your turn to regale us with a tune,' said Mr Pringle, looking over at Jane and me from his chair.

'Oh no—' I began.

'Come now, I won't take no for an answer.'

'Mr Pringle, I play very poorly!' I protested, determined to set him straight about my pianoforte skills.

'We are all friends here,' Mr Austen intoned. 'Why not try at least?'

'Oh yes, Flissy, do!' said Jane. There were murmurs of agreement from everyone else, and I started to feel slightly panicked. I didn't even have a notion of what tune I could play!

'Ahem.' I looked up, and Mr Humbleton was standing beside me with his arm proffered. 'Do not fear, Miss Felicity. I will escort you to the instrument and remain by your side to turn the pages.'

Mr Fitzroy had said nothing throughout this discussion but was surveying the scene with a sardonic smile. It made me determined to wipe it off his face despite being unsure my pianoforte skills were up to the task.

'Thank you, cousin. That is kind of you.' I took his arm, and we promenaded over to the pianoforte for all the world as if I was going to be providing a stellar performance (which I knew I was not!). I sat down on the bench and arranged my skirt. My heart was thudding at having to play for so many people; my palms too were clammy, and my fingers stiff with fear.

Mr Humbleton picked up the music book and studied it intently for a time. 'Might I suggest this tune?' he said eventually and pointed to his chosen song. I looked at it: 'The Lass of Richmond Hill'. 'It is, I think, the simplest of the lot,' he added in a low voice intended only for my ears.

I was grateful for him choosing a song that I could not destroy too much in the playing, and indeed, it was one that I knew and had played before. Perhaps this would not be too much of an ordeal after all.

I poised my fingers over the keys ... and began.

From the outset, I knew I was in trouble. My timing was off, playing far too quickly for Mr Humbleton to realise I'd come to the end of the page, so I was forced to make up the missing notes until he turned it. It didn't help that he was tapping his foot and humming under his breath, which really put me off my rhythm (what I had of it). Halfway through, to my horror, he decided he would help me out even further by singing the words!

This lass so neat, with smiles so sweet,
Has won my right good will;
I'd crowns resign to call her mine,
Sweet lass of Richmond Hill.

If Mr Humbleton's singing was superior to my playing, it could have helped us considerably—sadly, he was off-key, compounding the sorry state of affairs. Even worse was him actually leaning in and singing to me as if I were his sweet lass!

My cheeks burned as his voice rose to a fever pitch on the chorus: 'Sweet lass of Richmond Hiiiillll ...' and I crashed the final chords in an attempt to drown him out.

At the conclusion, I stood to a smattering of applause, relieved the hideous show was over. I risked a look at Jane and Harriet, and they were struggling to suppress their merriment. Mr Austen wore the face of someone in pain. Henry was smirking. Aunt and Mrs Austen were grimacing in sympathy, and Mr Pringle looked faintly horrified.

Only Papa, having bequeathed his tin ear to me, seemed to have enjoyed it and was creating the one-man applause. Then a slow clap joined him from the other side of the room.

I hadn't dared look at Mr Fitzroy once during the performance, but I did so now, reluctantly. He was leaning forward in his chair with a mischievous smirk on his annoying face.

'I enjoyed that immensely, Miss Blackburn,' he drawled. 'Can we have another? It was *so* very accomplished.'

I smiled thinly at him.

'Unfortunately, I will have to decline, Mr Fitzroy. It takes a lot of passion to perform such a complicated piece, and I'm afraid I've rather overexerted myself.'

'I am sorry to hear that,' he replied. 'And what a pity, as your playing was such a pleasurable experience.'

'I can only hope to give you the same pleasure at a future gathering.'

His lips twitched. 'I look forward to it.'

I bowed, and he returned it with a slow nod. I took the arm of Mr Humbleton, who seemed rather confused at this exchange, and yanked him away from the pianoforte.

What a nightmare; thankfully, Mr Austen decided that everyone's ears needed a thorough cleansing after my terrible playing and gladly took his seat at the instrument to play a sweet hymn.

I returned to my seat on the sofa next to Jane, and I could feel her quaking with laughter. 'Oh, Flissy!'

'Don't,' I whispered back miserably. 'Just don't!'

After that, the evening wrapped up remarkably quickly, with Mr Pringle pleading that he needed his beauty sleep. But as we were herded to our waiting carriage, he promised to call on Papa shortly to be measured for a new suit. I was hoping, for Harriet's sake, that this was an indication of him wanting to deepen his acquaintance with her also.

Seeing her expectant air and knowing she was not able to ask for propriety's sake, I suggested that perhaps he could be measured speedily and partake of tea and cake with us for the remainder of his visit. He replied that it sounded like a splendid idea, and Harriet immediately brightened and happily sprung into the carriage.

Mr Fitzroy had followed behind to see us off, out of politeness no doubt. But to my way of thinking, he need not have bothered. I was last to be loaded in, having hung back for as long as possible to breathe the cool night air, when a deep voice murmured by my shoulder, 'Allow me to assist.'

I looked down to find one of Mr Fitzroy's hands outstretched before me, as if in a peace offering. Hesitating a moment, I placed my ungloved hand in his, and he easily lifted me into the carriage. The touch and press of his warm skin against mine sent an electric thrill through my entire body.

'Thank you,' I said dazedly, and he inclined his head.

The carriage moved off with Mr Pringle, one hand held aloft, waving at us like he was the king. Mr Fitzroy stood beside him stern-faced and most decidedly not waving. But I watched carefully and saw again his hand, the one that had touched me, flex slowly just once. Then he walked away to the house without a backwards glance.

Chapter 7

I slept late the next morning and woke feeling tired and out of sorts. My head ached from the wine I'd drunk last night, and I'd had disturbing dreams, though I couldn't now remember what they were. Harriet was up and breakfasting when I slid into the dining room. Papa wasn't there, and neither was Mr Humbleton, thank goodness.

Harriet tsked when I declined a serving of scrambled eggs from the sideboard. 'Eating something substantial might help?'

I shook my head and lightly buttered a roll. 'Just this and a cup of tea will do.'

'I didn't think you had drunk that much.'

I bit into my roll and chewed. 'I had another couple of glasses in quick succession after the pianoforte fiasco,' I mumbled.

Harriet chuckled.

'Where is Papa and the songbird, might I ask?'

'They ate earlier and have gone into town,' she said. 'Apparently, our cousin wanted some exercise and to discuss something with Papa.'

Unconcerned about this information, I poured my tea and thought nothing of it.

Mary appeared at the door and bobbed. 'Letter for you, Miss Harriet.'

She handed over a small white envelope with a silver wafer seal, and Harriet snatched it up. It was addressed to 'Miss Harriet Blackburn' in swirling cursive. Mr Pringle's handwriting, I detected.

'Oh, Fliss, it's from him.'

'Indeed. Well, you'd better open it and see what he says.'

'I can't!' she gasped.

'Give it here then.'

I wiped my buttery fingers on a napkin, took the letter from her, and scanned the contents. 'He plans to call on you at two o'clock this afternoon. There is no mention of being measured for a suit unless it has been arranged already with Papa. From this letter, it seems you are the sole intention of his visit.'

Harriet let out a small squawk of joy, and I smiled and handed the letter to her, which she clasped to her bosom. Indeed, I could not help but be pleased for her after all she had endured on Mr Pringle's account.

'Oh, happy day,' she swooned.

'He hasn't proposed yet,' I cautioned. 'We shouldn't get our hopes up. He may just want to borrow a book.'

She gave me a withering glance.

'But', I added, 'You were obviously in his thoughts since he was up with the larks penning that epistle. All indications lead to him liking you very much indeed.'

'I hope so,' she breathed. 'We must find you someone, Flissy, now that you are free of any arrangement with Samuel.'

'I am perfectly content, thank you,' I murmured, sipping my tea and doing my best not to think of Mr Stonyface's proud countenance. I stared out the window as if seeing the sun for the first time. 'It is such a lovely day. I think I shall follow our cousin's example and stroll to the lake for some fresh air.'

'But you will be back before two o'clock to chaperone?' Harriet said, her tone anxious.

'Of course, dearest. I shall be back before you know I've gone.'

Leaving Harriet to fuss over her wardrobe and determine which dress might most please Mr Pringle's discerning gaze, I pulled on my bonnet and strode off to the lake. We called it a 'lake', but in truth, it was more of a pond.

It was a mere half-mile walk, but the day was a fine one—and hot. After traversing several open fields, I reached a small copse, through which I knew a stream ran.

Mopping my face with my handkerchief, I stopped for a breather and crouched down, cupping my hand under the flow of water to take a well-earned ice-cold drink. Wiping my hand on my skirt, I continued on in no hurry, ambling along the shady path and listening to the birds chirping and rustling in the trees. I found escaping into nature to be a soothing balm whenever I felt troubled.

In this case, it was two men causing me consternation. Mr Humbleton's insistent attention to me was starting to grate, and I longed for his visit to be over or for Cassie to arrive home—whichever happened first. But that situation was like trying to close a warped cupboard door; no matter how hard I pressed to shut it neatly, the edges wouldn't meet. I would just have to be patient and sow the seeds of her kindness and beauty and hope he took the bait.

Then there was the itch that was Mr Fitzroy. For someone I barely knew, he seemed to have inserted himself quite firmly and vividly into my life within a matter of weeks. His presence irked and intrigued me in equal measure and, I couldn't deny it, attracted me. In general, him being tall, dark, handsome, and wealthy was enough to entice any woman, myself included; and if his nature had been more cheerful, then he would have made a desirable package indeed.

However, I disliked his irascible manner and found it

annoying and uncalled for. What reason did he have for being so surly when he was rich and handsome? It made no sense to me.

But last night, he'd shown another side to his temperament, one that appreciated a humorous situation and enjoyed witty conversation. That had been a surprise. Then the touch of his hand sparking such a reaction in me had been another. I knew not what to make of him now at all, whether I should be open to what other surprises he might have in store or stay well away from him.

It was with these musings on my mind that I came out of the trees and headed down the narrow dirt path to the edge of the lake.

Wandering over to my favourite shady rock, I was about to unlace my shoes to dip my toes in the water when I spied a neatly folded pile of clothes and a pair of well-polished black boots. But no accompanying body.

Shading my eyes, I scanned the horizon and saw the dark head of a man (I assumed it was a man judging by the pair of folded breeches) bobbing in the distance.

How annoying! I'd walked here specifically to have some solitary time, and now someone else had gotten here first and stolen my respite. Well, I wasn't going to be the one forced to go. I shaded my eyes again and realised the person (whoever it was) had seen me and was now swimming speedily in my direction. It was only when their face came into focus that I realised exactly who it was. Despite the heat of the day, my blood ran cold, then fizzed hotly in my veins. Mr Fitzroy, with his wet hair plastered against his forehead, was swimming through the glistening waters of the lake towards me and, if the neat pile of clothing was anything to go by, completely naked.

The delicious feeling of having the upper hand overtook my senses and made me giddy. *Finally,* I thought, *I have him at my mercy.* This was going to be most excellent fun and a sound payback for commenting on my humiliating pianoforte performance!

'Good day, Miss Blackburn!' gasped the man when he was within hailing distance, his face red from the exertion of swimming or perhaps sunburn. He seemed to be treading water and rather reluctant to stand up straight.

'Good day, Mr Fitzroy!' I returned merrily. 'A lovely day for a swim, is it not?'

'Er, yes. I did not expect that anyone would venture here. Otherwise, I would not have ... disrobed. Please forgive me.'

My eyes flicked towards his pile of clothing. 'Quite.'

'If you would be so kind as to leave ...'

'Leave? Why would I leave? I've only just arrived after an arduous walk, and I'm rather tired, so I'd like to rest awhile.'

I sat down firmly on the rock by the shore and rested my back against a tree, as if I were going to be there a good long while. (I actually needed to start making my way back to play chaperone to Harriet relatively soonish. But he didn't need to know that!)

Mr Fitzroy blinked at me and swept a hand through his short dark hair to push it out of his eyes. It stuck up in front like a duck's tail. I could see from his expression that he was flummoxed and unsure how to proceed and, by the way he was shivering slightly, that he was also desperate to get out of the water. The lake was never warm, even at the height of summer. It was fed from an underground spring that came from deep in the earth. Truth be told, I was surprised he'd managed to stay in for this long.

I watched him weigh up the situation carefully as to what to do without losing his composure or his dignity, and I knew exactly the two choices he had open to him. He could keep swimming until I grew bored and left or stride from the water with his naked body on display.

The hairs on the back of my neck bristled in anticipation. For all his crotchetiness, Mr Fitzroy was an incredibly handsome gentleman; and I, for one, would not complain if the latter was the route he decided to take.

'Well', he said eventually, 'would you mind awfully if you closed your eyes?'

Ah, excellent! He had chosen the latter!

'But it is such a lovely day, and the view is lovely from where I'm sitting,' I said idly, swinging my foot. 'I wouldn't want to miss a second of it. So why would I close my eyes?'

Mr Fitzroy's mouth pinched, and his brows furrowed, and I could tell he was struggling to keep his temper.

'Miss Blackburn, you are being deliberately provoking.'

'Not at all. Besides, shouldn't you like to swim for a bit longer? The day is so warm,' I added with a small smile.

'No, I'm rather cold actually and would like to g-get out!' It was true that his lips were turning a faint shade of purple, and his teeth were starting to chatter.

I relented slightly. Mr Fitzroy freezing to death wouldn't be a good thing to have on my conscience.

'It seems we are at an impasse,' I said. 'I want to stay here with my eyes open. You want your clothing. The only thing that stands between us is your ... indecency.' I coughed delicately and fanned my face as if an innocent young maiden.

Mr Fitzroy's eyes narrowed, and his nostrils flared.

'So what d-do you p-propose?' he chatter-growled.

'I could throw you your shirt, with a rock in it.'

'That is your idea of a compromise?' he said disbelievingly.

'Yes. I can throw it so it plops in the water near you.'

I demonstrated the action with a flip of my hand for dramatic effect. 'All you have to do is retrieve the item and put it on, and voilà! Neither one of us has to be inconvenienced.'

He sighed. 'Very well. But m-make h-haste.'

Smiling to myself, I took up his shirt, made a bit of a show of shaking it out, and looked around for a largish rock. Spying a round smooth one that I thought might do the trick, I held it aloft so he could see. He nodded sharply and pressed his lips together, looking annoyed. It was all I could do to stop from giggling aloud. I couldn't wait to share this with Jane. I knew she would be in fits of laughter.

Deliberately slowly, I placed the rock in the middle of his shirt, folded it over, and tied the arms tightly to fashion a kind of parcel. That done, I stood on the shore, did a couple of preparatory swings, and heaved it towards him. I wasn't worried about hitting him because I knew my aim was pretty horrendous. I'd once played cricket with Jane and her brothers, and the balls I bowled went nowhere near the direction of the stumps.

Still, on this occasion, he did have to jerk back as the shirt parcel sailed rather close to his head before hitting the water with a resounding splash.

'Oops, sorry!' I called out and sat down again to await the next bit of fun: Mr Fitzroy trying to undo the shirt from the rock and then attempting to put it on while still in the water.

I heard him mutter several expletives as he fished out the rock and fiddled with the arms of the shirt.

'I hope you're not having difficulty?' I enquired.

'I'm p-perfectly f-fine,' he answered through gritted teeth, his face mottled.

Finally, he got it untied and floated the shirt out before him in the water. Trying to put a waterlogged shirt over one's head was no mean feat. So to rouse his spirits, I called encouragement from the shore as he attempted to get his head in the opening.

'That's it! Oh dear, try again! You almost had it!'

By now, I would have thought he would just give up and come out, but he was so stubborn!

After half a dozen tries, he managed to duck his head into the opening and emerged triumphantly, spitting a stream of water.

'Bravo!' I called and gave him a clap.

Mr Fitzroy, his jaw set in annoyance, emerged out of the lake a dripping wet Poseidon, the once-white (and now slightly mud-streaked) shirt clinging to his form. I gaped as I beheld that the transparent shirt that hung to midthigh didn't really do much to conceal his manhood. He realised the same thing too late and hastily turned his back to me.

But the clear outline of his firm buttocks under the see-through material was quite another view entirely and most pleasing to behold.

'My breeches and jacket, if you please,' he muttered, holding out his hand.

'Certainly,' I replied, passing his clothes to him and making no attempt to look away as he pulled his breeches on, covering those fine fleshly specimens out of sight.

'Have you had enough of a show?' Mr Fitzroy turned and gave me a withering look.

'Do not mind me. I've seen it all before,' I said breezily, then realised what kind of light that painted me in. 'Er, I mean, in a human anatomy book, of course. In my opinion, you have nothing to be ashamed of.'

Mr Fitzroy's face flushed bright red. 'Boots!' he barked at me, and I silently handed them to him, thinking his attitude was rather uncalled for. Hadn't I given him a compliment?

After jamming his wet feet into his boots with a loud squeaking noise, he straightened.

'Good day, Miss Blackburn. I would say it was a pleasure seeing you, but it has been most decidedly *not!*' Without waiting for a reply or even bowing, he turned on his heel and strode off up the path.

'You forgot your ...!' I called after him. 'Hat.'

But he was gone. *How rude!* I thought.

Feeling a little less inclined to laugh after Mr Fitzroy's aggressive departure, I snatched up his hat and plonked it on top of my bonnet. It would make an excellent birdbath for the robins that visited our back garden!

After that excitement, I hastened back as fast as I could. It wasn't easy walking quickly with a top hat on my head; it kept slipping off! Fearing that I had spent far too long engaging with Mr Fitzroy at the pond and that Harriet's chance with Mr Pringle would be ruined, I clutched the hat by its brim and ran.

When I reached the house, there was no sign of a carriage outside, and I dashed up the front path.

'Harriet!' I called from the hallway.

She came out from the parlour in a flurry, looking pristine in a pale-pink silk dress that matched her cheeks. Her golden hair was sleek and pinned up with an array of glossy curls framing her face.

'Fliss! I've nearly chewed my nails ragged! Where have you been? And why are you holding a top hat?'

I started to tell her, but she interrupted.

'Don't mind that now! He should be here within five minutes! You don't have time to change, but please tidy your hair and clean your face at least!'

She swept off back to the parlour. Feeling contrite, I raced upstairs, threw the hat on my bed, yanked off my bonnet, and attempted to re-pin my hair. I scrubbed at my face with a white washcloth, which came away grime streaked, reminding me of Mr Fitzroy's shirt. Our encounter had fired me up no end. What an abominable man!

Chapter 8

On the dot of two o'clock, we heard clopping outside, and there was a faint 'Whoa, boy!' I peeked out the window from behind the parlour curtain and saw a gentleman dismounting from his horse.

'It's him. It's Mr Pringle!' I hissed.

Harriet's eyes widened. She stood up, then at once sat down again and wrung her hands.

'Zounds! I don't know what to do with myself. Is he really here?'

'Indeed.'

'Now you don't need to be concerned. Just act natural!'

'I am, dearest,' I said, amused, 'Are you telling that to me or yourself?'

There was a knock at the parlour door. Harriet sat up poker straight on the sofa, her hands clasped in her lap.

'Come in,' she intoned in a regal voice, which made me want to giggle.

The door opened, and Mary appeared. 'A Mr Pringle is here to see you, miss.'

'Very good, Mary. Please show him in and bring us

through some tea presently.'

She bobbed a curtsy. 'Of course, miss.'

Harriet whispered to me, 'I hope he likes scones. I asked Sue to whip up a batch while you were out. We can have them with jam and cream.'

It had been a while since my single bread roll at breakfast, and I'd missed luncheon, so scones sounded excellent. My stomach gurgled loudly in anticipation, and Harriet shot me a look of abject horror.

But she didn't have time to scold as Mr Pringle strode into the room with a wide smile. We stood immediately, and he bowed to Harriet. 'Miss Blackburn.' Then he turned and did the same for me. 'Miss Blackburn.'

We bowed in unison to return the greeting.

'Mr Pringle, do come in and take a seat. How was your journey?' Harriet's voice was smooth, and I marvelled that she was all of a sudden poised and elegant. It rubbed off on me somewhat, and I found myself sinking to the sofa carefully rather than flopping on it like I usually did. Mr Pringle was gentry, after all, and I didn't want him reporting anything back to his abominable friend. So I needed to be on my best behaviour.

'My ride was very pleasant, thank you,' he replied, sitting down and flicking his coat-tails out of the way. 'Apart from the newly harvested hay in the fields quite setting me off into a fit of sneezing. I have an allergy, you see,' he explained.

'Oh dear!' Harriet said, her face a picture of concern. 'Do you need me to fetch you something?'

A big handkerchief probably, I thought, looking at his watery eyes and red nose.

'No, no, I will cope,' he said, sniffling. 'Nothing a cup of tea won't fix. I say, this is a jolly parlour.' He looked around the room, and his gaze landed on our pianoforte in the corner. But he deliberately avoided mentioning it (no doubt in case I suggested performing) and instead chose to comment politely on other less traumatic aspects.

'I do like the purple wallpaper and the nook over there with the armchairs surrounding the fireplace. It must be very cosy in winter.'

'Yes, it is the warmest room in the house. Papa often jokes that he will move his bed in here,' said Harriet.

'Speaking of your father, I thought I might have a word with him afterwards, if I may?'

Ah, so he did want a new suit, I thought. But he did not want Harriet to feel she was tacked on to that task, so he hadn't mentioned it in the letter. Very nicely done!

'He is out with our cousin at present,' I replied. 'However, we expect them back shortly.'

What was taking Papa so long? I doubted it was for love

of our cousin's company. Perhaps he had taken Mr Humbleton visiting around the parish? But why do that if he was leaving next week?

There was a tap at the door, and Mary entered with a tray that held the tea-things, along with a cake stand of scones. Mr Pringle's eyes brightened. 'Ooh, scones!' he exclaimed.

'Yes, I had our cook make them specially for your visit,' said Harriet, smiling and tilting her head towards him. 'I hope you will partake in one or two?'

'Thank you, I shall indeed. I adore scones,' said Mr Pringle politely and proceeded to load a plate with several.

I watched anxiously in case he partook of too many. I intended to eat at least three ...

When he had finished preparing his scones with the accompaniments, Harriet nodded at me and began to pour the tea. Grateful to be finally let loose on them, I chose a big scone, split it in two, then slathered each half with butter and jam and added two generous dollops of cream. I took a large bite out of one half and hummed with enjoyment, not caring that I now had cream all over my nose.

Mr Pringle chuckled. 'That is how it is done, I see.'

'Felicity!' Harriet had noticed my gutsiness, and I hastily wiped my face with a napkin. 'Do excuse my sister's manners, Mr Pringle.'

'Not at all.' He promptly added another spoonful of cream to his half-eaten scone and bit into it with relish, earning a dashing cream moustache.

I was delighted at him following my lead. I was beginning to like Mr Pringle immensely; he was so much more fun than his friend. 'See, Harriet, it is the only way to eat scones,' I said with a laugh.

Mr Pringle merely smiled at Harriet's tsking and took the cup of tea she handed him. He wiped his mouth with a napkin and said, 'Tell me, Miss Blackburn ...'

'Oh, please, do call us Miss Felicity and Miss Harriet,' I begged him. 'It will make it easier to know who you are addressing.'

'Very well, Miss Felicity. Do you often visit the pond that lies between our two houses?'

'On occasion,' I replied warily, unsure as to where his line of questioning was going and who it might involve.

'I only ask because I had the most interesting conversation with my friend Max. He was striding up the drive in a foul temper as I set off on my horse. Upon spying that his shirt was muddy and sopping wet, I enquired as to what had occurred, and his reply was quite extraordinary!'

I shifted uncomfortably at hearing this and concentrated on sipping my tea.

Harriet supplied the necessary question to prompt our

guest. 'So what did he say?'

'He said, and I quote, "I was detained in the pond by Miss Felicity Blackburn." Then without another word, he stamped into the house! Most peculiar. As I was already on my way here, I thought I might enquire as to the origins of my friend's vexation."

Harriet's eyes were upon me. 'Fliss, what did you do to poor Mr Fitzroy?'

I nearly scoffed at that; there was no 'poor Mr Fitzroy' about it.

They were both looking at me curiously, so I took another sip of tea and a bite of scone and, after swallowing both, summarised the event.

'It was of no consequence, really. I simply happened upon Mr Fitzroy swimming in the pond—without clothes.'

Harriet gasped, her hand flying to her mouth. Mr Pringle grinned. 'Ah, I see. How inconvenient for him.'

'Yes, and for me since I had just arrived and wished to relax on my favourite shady rock. We determined a compromise in that I tossed him his shirt, he put it on, and then he was able to exit the pond with decorum ...'

In my mind's eye, I saw again very plainly the wondrous sight of Mr Fitzroy emerging from the water—how his broad muscled chest had heaved with exertion, how his sodden shirt had clung to his shapely upper thighs, and, even though the lake was freezing, how he'd been delightfully well endowed ...

I swallowed and added, 'That was the end of it. I don't see why he needed to be so grumpy. Most countrymen I know would simply laugh it off.'

Mr Pringle looked at me for a moment as if weighing up his next words carefully. 'There are a few things I can divulge about my friend that may help to explain his temperament. I trust this information will not be made public knowledge?'

'Of course,' said Harriet instantly. 'We don't make a habit of spreading gossip, do we, Fliss?'

I shook my head, thinking of Jane and some of the conversations we'd had recently. Well, it wasn't spreading gossip as such ...

'Max's parents, though rich and respected in society, didn't have much time for him,' began Mr Pringle solemnly. 'He was the youngest of seven children, and as you can imagine, their patience had quite run dry with demands from the other six ...'

Mr Pringle finished the rest of his scone and declared, 'I must say, these are the best scones I have eaten in a long while. Please do give my compliments to your cook.' Then he settled back in his chair, crossing his legs at the ankle.

Harriet beamed. 'I shall! Would you like another cup of tea?'

'I believe I should,' he said, smiling at her, and she blushed.

Come on, I thought impatiently. *Stop flirting with Harriet and tell us the rest of the story.* I cleared my throat. 'You were saying ... about Mr Fitzroy?'

'Oh, yes. Max was packed off to boarding school at a young age. He saw his family only during term holidays and Christmas and sometimes not even then if his parents were travelling on the Continent. I'm afraid they rather liked their own company and found their children to be tiresome.'

'Sounds a bit like Jane's family,' I commented. 'Her brother Edward was adopted out to relations because there were too many of them to look after.'

'Though you couldn't say that Mr and Mrs Austen don't care about their children,' interjected Harriet. 'More loving parents you will never meet. It was simply a matter of not being able to provide for them all.'

'Indeed,' said Mr Pringle, nodding as if he understood what it was like to have too many mouths to feed and not enough income (I doubted he did). 'Anyway,' he continued, 'the upshot of the matter is that because he spent so much time alone, Max has the unfortunate disadvantage of not having, shall we say, the ease of conversing with people he doesn't know well. But I assure you once you get past the stern facade and his good opinion is secured, he is a most loyal friend and the most wonderful company.'

I should have to take Mr Pringle's word about that since he was his friend after all. But hearing about Mr Fitzroy's sterile upbringing did explain why his disposition was so gruff. I had thought him unfriendly, but perhaps it was just a mask for protection?

Hearing Mr Pringle sing his praises so thoroughly made me feel contrite about teasing him at the lake. No wonder he hadn't known what to do in that situation or been able to 'laugh it off'. Plus I still hadn't apologised for my behaviour in the carriage that day from Overton. What he must think of me ...

'Do you think Mr Fitzroy would perhaps ... Would he be open to ... a letter of apology?' I asked hesitantly. 'I wouldn't like him to think ill of my behaviour or to bear a grudge against me.'

Indeed now, strangely, I felt I needed to do the utmost to win back his favour!

I waited anxiously as Mr Pringle frowned and considered, tapping his finger slightly against his teacup. 'I think that a well-written letter would go some way to dispel any animosity on his part,' he said at last. 'It is true that he doesn't forgive easily when wronged, and it would be awkward for future gatherings if not resolved quickly, especially as I'm thinking of holding a ball at Ashbury. What do you think? Would it be well received?'

Harriet let out a small squeal of delight. 'Oh yes, Mr Pringle, a ball would be wonderful!'

'Excellent! And please do call me Evan if we are to be on a first-name basis.'

'All right ... Evan,' Harriet said, blushing prettily.

Mr Pringle, or Evan, as I supposed I should have to call him now, inclined his head to her with a smile.

I rolled my eyes a little at the performance. It was obvious that he was very interested in my sister, and she in him.

It struck me suddenly that he might indeed propose to her, and Harriet would happily accept. And then she would move out to live with him and become mistress of the manor here, in London, or wherever he chose. That was a strange thought indeed, and it took me by surprise. I had been readily helping her to achieve a good match but not considering the reality—that she might get her wish. And then I would no longer have her here to talk and laugh with whenever I wanted. This was a selfish way of thinking; of course I wanted Harriet to be happy, but I couldn't help but feel a little sorry for myself at the same time as it meant that I would be left alone with Papa—a spinster!

As I mused about my fate and what would become of me, Harriet and Evan conversed happily about books they liked. Then there was the sound of heavy footsteps in the hallway, and Papa entered the room without knocking.

'Oh, Mr Pringle,' he said with an expression of surprise. 'Forgive my absence. I didn't realise you were to visit us today.' He gave a quick bow.

Evan stood and returned it.

'Not at all, sir. It was a whim of mine early this morning at breakfast. I sent my footman over with a hastily scribbled note with my intention to call upon your daughter ... Miss Harriet.' He smiled at her, and she gazed up at him, clearly smitten.

'Ah, I see,' said Papa, witnessing the attraction between the two lovebirds.

'I've been playing chaperone, Papa,' I said. 'And consuming scones.'

'Indeed,' Papa said with a chuckle, seating himself across from me in an armchair. 'Now what have you all been discussing?'

'Mr Pringle, Evan, wishes to hold a ball at Ashbury,' said Harriet excitedly.

'Does he? Well, that is good news. I might get some commissions from gentlemen requiring new suits if that is the case.'

'Since I am here, perhaps I might take a little of your time to be measured for one?' said Evan. 'After you've had refreshment, of course.'

'Yes, that is an excellent idea,' said Papa, looking pleased at the request. Harriet rang for Mary, and she came and took the teapot and the cake stand away to refill after I'd made a grab for the last scone.

'Where is our cousin?' I asked as I buttered my scone, hoping against hope that he'd left suddenly without the need to say goodbye.

'He is rather tired after our excursion in the village. So he has retired to your, er, his room to relax and read his Bible.'

Papa looked at me carefully for a long moment as I took a large bite out of my scone, but I didn't wonder too much why he was. No doubt he thought me rude for commandeering the last one without offering half of it to him, or I had cream on my nose again!

Chapter 9

Dear Mr Fitzroy,

I do hope you have recovered from your swim with no ill effects. After our meeting at the lake the other day, I cannot stop thinking about how fetching you looked in your wet shirt

No, no, that wouldn't do at all! I scrunched up that letter, took a clean sheet of paper, cleared my mind, and began again.

Dear Mr Fitzroy,

This letter may seem forward, but I would like to apologise for my manner in the carriage from Overton last week when you were kind enough to offer my sister and me a ride home.

Furthermore, my behaviour at the lake the other day was most unladylike, and I fear I may have said some things that were out of turn and may have caused you offence.

I do hope you can forgive me for both incidents in question and bear me no ill will and that we can converse in the spirit of friendship at future social events.

Yours most sincerely,
Miss Felicity Blackburn

PS: I have your hat.

There, it was done!

I blotted the ink, read it over a couple of times, and then a couple more for good measure. Wanting a second opinion, I left our bedroom and went in search of Harriet. It was the day after Mr Pringle's visit, and she'd been floating around the house and not able to settle on any particular task. I found her in the dining room, snipping the ends off some cornflowers and arranging them in a vase with a dreamy look on her face.

'Can you have a look at my letter? I'm about to send it to Mr Fitzroy, and I need to make sure I haven't said anything that will cause him further offence.'

Harriet wiped her hands on her apron and took it from me. After perusing it, she handed it back. 'It is brief, but to the point, which I think he will appreciate. He doesn't seem like a man who would endure long-windedness.'

'No, that is what I thought. I couldn't allude to any of the information that Mr Pringle shared with us in private as it might suggest that is what prompted me to write it in the first place, hence why it is so short. Is that a bad thing? Maybe I should expand it.' I felt anxious all of a sudden that Mr Fitzroy would not be soothed by my apology and be riled up even more.

Harriet placed a hand on my arm. 'It is a good letter, Fliss. Do not fret. I think if you write something longer, the true intention would be lost. I believe it should be well received. And thank you for writing it. After all, you may have to keep company with him in the future if Mr Pringle ... Evan ... proposes.'

Her tone was confident to the point that if she'd said '*when* he proposes', I wouldn't have been surprised. But it seemed Harriet wasn't counting her chickens before they'd hatched—outwardly at least.

'Where did all these flowers come from?' I asked, watching as she added a bunch of meadowsweet to the arrangement.

'Mr Humbleton was out walking early this morning and gathered them.'

'Oh.'

I readied myself to walk into Steventon to take the letter to the post shop for the afternoon delivery. I was in the hallway, tucking a stray strand of hair into my bonnet, when a figure loomed behind me in the mirror.

Startled, I turned to find Mr Humbleton hovering with an expectant look on his face. My heart sank. *Please, God, don't let him want to chat*, I prayed. *I won't make the post.*

'Cousin.' I nodded to him and edged towards the front door. 'I'm afraid I have urgent business in town—'

'I won't keep you,' he intervened. 'But might I present you with this small token?'

From behind his back, he produced a posy of flowers, the same cornflowers and meadowsweet that Harriet had been arranging. It was tied with a yellow ribbon.

My eyes narrowed. Had he asked her to make it for him? If so, why had she not said? No, I suspected he had been labouring at the task in secret up in his room with myself as its unwary beneficiary.

Reluctantly, I took the posy that he proffered as what else could I do?

'Thank you,' I said, quite at a loss as to what to say or do next.

Luckily, that was solved for me. With his cheeks reddening, my cousin bowed and mumbled, 'Good day, Miss Felicity.' Then he scarpered up the stairs, leaving me to gaze in frustration after him.

Mr Humbleton's attention was not just grating, it was now decidedly worrying. First the off-key singing, now the flowers. It appeared he had formed a one-sided attachment and was indeed pursuing me without any encouragement!

Much disturbed, I plonked the posy in a vase on the sideboard, leaving it to its unwatered fate, and exited the house.

I was so caught up in my own thoughts all the way into town that I nearly bumped into Jane coming out of the post shop as I was entering.

'Hello! What good timing. I was just thinking about you. I was posting a letter to Cassie.' She made to grasp me on the arm and kiss my cheek but paused, seeing I wasn't in good spirits. 'What has happened? You look like you need cheering up.'

'Oh, indeed I do. Just let me post this.'

I took the letter from my pocket and we went back into the post shop.

'Who are you writing to?' she asked curiously.

'Mr Fitzroy. As penance for my sins,' I said in a low voice.

She lifted an eyebrow. 'Do tell.'

'Not here,' I whispered with a quick glance at the postmistress, who was sorting mail for the afternoon delivery behind the counter. Mrs Sutton was a notorious gossip. It was bad enough that she would see I was writing to Mr Fitzroy, but what else I had to say would be a veritable feast for her ears.

But I dutifully handed over my letter and whisked Jane out of the shop before the woman could ask any probing questions.

When we were well out of earshot, I invited Jane to come home with me for luncheon, and she readily agreed. 'My eyes need a rest. I've been writing nonstop this morning.'

'Cassie's letter?' I asked. 'You've been writing to her a lot lately.'

'That and other jottings,' she replied after a moment's pause. 'Anyway, tell me what's been happening. Why are you writing to Mr Fitzroy?'

As we strolled down the lane arm in arm, past the open fields, the scent of newly harvested hay drifted to my nose, reminding me of Mr Pringle's sneezing fit. I wondered how much I should reveal of what he had said about Mr Fitzroy's upbringing. I decided to err on the side of caution.

'I'm attempting to get along with him for Harriet's sake. I came across him bathing at the pond yesterday, and I'm afraid I rather made fun of him.'

'Oh dear. How exactly?'

'He wanted me to leave, and I insisted that I wouldn't. I

said that the only way he could come out of the water decorously was for me to throw him his shirt with a rock in it.'

Jane chuckled. 'I would have loved to have seen that! Did he glower at you?'

'He did, quite ferociously! But he managed to put the thing on after half a dozen attempts. Then he emerged, and I didn't try too hard to avert my eyes. I may have commented quite boldly on his ... appendage.'

'Flissy!'

'I know, it was most unladylike. But it was right there and difficult to ignore. He was not best pleased, even though I was complimentary.'

'I'm sure.' Jane sounded like she was struggling to keep a straight face. 'Oh, how I wish I had been there hiding in a bush to witness that. I can picture the displeased look on his face so clearly!' She chortled with glee.

'I knew you would laugh. I think it was the thought of telling you about it that spurred me on.'

'You can't blame me for your deplorable behaviour! I assume the letter is to smooth his ruffled feathers?'

'Indeed. Mr Pringle, or Evan, as he told us to call him, took tea with us yesterday and seems quite enraptured with Harriet. So I felt it my duty to reconcile with his irascible friend and write him an apologetic letter for whatever good it may do. Oh well, it is sent now.'

Jane tightened her grip on my arm. 'No matter. Let him make of it what he will. But that is good news about Harriet. I am so pleased for her, especially after that hiccup when he went away.'

I smiled. 'You will see for yourself how she blooms.' My smile faltered. 'Speaking of blooms, I received a posy from our cousin before I left for town this morning. I confess I am worried about what he intends by it.'

'He does seem rather taken with you, if his singing the other night was anything to go by.'

'It is not from any encouragement on my end, I assure you,' I returned hotly.

'I know.'

'Honestly, I'm beginning to think that he might actually go down on bended knee, and I do NOT want to marry the man.'

'What has your father said?'

'Nothing.'

'Well, it may just be a passing fancy in Mr Humbleton's head, and he will not take action.'

'I don't suppose I could distract him with talk of Cassie? She may think him a worthy suitor when she returns ...'

'Definitely not!' said Jane, sounding horrified. 'I know he is your cousin, but I don't want him as a brother-in-law!'

So that put an axe in the neck of my plan, but I couldn't blame her.

'My advice is to do your best to thwart his advances for the rest of his visit,' Jane continued reassuringly. 'Let us pray that he grows disillusioned and leaves before attempting any formal proposal.'

'Amen to that!' I exclaimed, and a cow in the adjoining field lifted her head and mooed loudly as if in agreement. We ran off down the road towards home, giggling like fiends, and I felt calmer about the situation. Jane always knew the right thing to say.

When we arrived, I deposited Jane in the dining room to natter with Harriet and went off to tell Sue there was an extra guest for luncheon plus check there was enough to eat. Now that we had Mr Humbleton staying with us, we'd had to increase our expenditure where food was concerned. He didn't have a small appetite either.

Sue took the news graciously. 'I'll slice some more cold roast beef, miss. And there's plenty of boiled potatoes and greens.'

'Can we round it out with some bread rolls and butter too, perhaps?'

She nodded. 'Yes, miss. I'll ask Mary to serve shortly.'

'Very good. Thank you, Sue.'

Upon entering the dining room, I was disconcerted to see Mr Humbleton was seated at the table and directly across from where I usually sat. He tended to take luncheon with Papa in his studio. But today, for some reason, he had decided to grace us with his presence. I sighed to myself. So much for a pleasant meal with my friend and my sister. Now we had to listen to him wittering on.

He was holding court with Jane and Harriet, and they were nodding politely as he told them of his visit around the parish and whom he had met. I still didn't know why he was bothering. Mr Pringle intended to hold his ball this Saturday, and Mr Humbleton was leaving a few days afterwards. So he hardly needed to make himself known in Steventon.

Mary came in with our plates of roast beef, potatoes, and greens, along with a dish of mustard; and the meal commenced. She'd just returned with a platter of bread rolls, which she placed in the middle of the table along with a slab of butter, when Mr Humbleton cleared his throat. 'Do allow me to butter you a roll, Miss Felicity.'

'That's quite all right,' I said, reaching for a roll at the same time he did. Our hands collided mid-air. His fingers were cold and clammy, like touching a dead fish; and I drew mine back instantly, feeling repelled. He took the opportunity to snatch a roll and place it on his plate.

I grasped the butter dish, but he took hold of the other side.

'I insist,' he said and proceeded to tug it towards him. I tugged back. There was a short, but sharp wrestling match, one that I was determined to win. But I didn't have a good-enough purchase, and he wrenched it away, triumphant.

I had to sit there silently and wait for him to butter the roll. When he was finished, he bowed and held the plate aloft, and I took the roll with a grudging 'Thank you'. How I hated him forcing me into a situation that felt vaguely intimate, especially when I was trying to thwart his advances! I wanted to give him no encouragement, not even the chance to butter me a roll!

Jane and Harriet were witness to this pantomime, and I knew they would be feeling sympathy for me (and also amusement). I would if I were them. I cut into my roast beef, hoping that he wouldn't ask if he could spread mustard for me too. Thankfully, he didn't offer.

We had just begun on a berry tart for afters when Mary popped her head in to say we had another visitor: Aunt Snelling. She always turned up at mealtimes, so she'd probably sniffed we were having luncheon, and it had taken her the first course to get ready and trot over.

'Please show her in, Mary, and bring another plate and spoon,' said Harriet, proceeding to cut a slice of berry tart.

Shortly, the lady herself entered and protested that she did not want any tart, then allowed that she would take a slice—but no cream.

'Mr Humbleton, Miss Austen. Gracious, there's quite the gathering here! And your father ...?'

'Papa is working,' Harriet replied, handing her a plate. 'He's been inundated with requests for new suits for Mr Pringle's ball on Saturday. Fliss and I may be required to help with stitching if his apprentices cannot keep up.'

'Gracious!' Aunt cut a spoonful of tart and popped it into her mouth. 'Actually, I will have a little cream, just to sweeten the flavour. Your cook has been too light-handed with the sugar.' She added a large dollop. 'Speaking of Mr Pringle, I heard something just now that concerned me greatly, and I thought I should come over straightaway and check the validity of it.'

'Oh?' Harriet leaned forward with a frown. 'He is not ill, is he?'

'No, no. It is not about him per se. It is about his friend, the stern-looking gentleman who is staying with him ...'

Her gaze turned to me, and my heart skipped a beat, having a notion of what was to follow.

'I've just heard, and from good authority,' she continued, 'that he is to receive a letter from Miss Felicity Blackburn this afternoon.'

I groaned inwardly and raised my eyebrows at Jane, and she shook her head slightly in commiseration. News did indeed travel like lightning here, thanks to the dedication of our postmistress to spread local gossip.

'I cannot fathom why you are writing to him, dear,' said Aunt, sounding perturbed. 'He is the most objectionable man I have ever encountered. So sour-faced!'

'I would like to know the same thing,' added Mr Humbleton in an accusatory tone. I felt like saying it was none of his business.

However, this could get back to Papa; and if he got wind of how I'd behaved with Mr Fitzroy, he might curtail my freedoms (such as they were). I had to come up with something—and quick. But for once, my mind went blank, and I could not think of a single reason as to why I might write to him.

'I ... Um ...'

'It is because of me,' supplied Jane hurriedly, seeing I was floundering. All eyes turned to her.

'You, Miss Austen?' said Aunt in surprise.

'I told him at supper the other night that he could borrow one of Father's books from the library. But then I remembered that I had lent it to Felicity ...'

I saw where she was going with this and gratefully picked up the thread. 'Yes, and I simply wrote a short note to let him know that I had finished with it and would bring it along to the ball on Saturday ...'

Blast! Now I would have to find a book to take!

'But there is a sizeable library at Ashbury,' said Aunt, sounding confused. 'Surely, he can find something to read in there?'

'It is a special edition ...' I trailed off lamely. 'I would not willingly write to him, but Jane asked me to as a courtesy.' *And neither would I again if it was to become public knowledge within a few hours!*

'I should hope not,' interjected Mr Humbleton. 'Especially when you are about to be my—' He stopped abruptly and cleared his throat. 'Please excuse me, ladies. I must talk to your father.' He got up from the table, addressed Aunt with a somewhat awkward bow, and practically ran from the room.

About to be his what? Alarm flooded my being, and I felt like I was hurtling towards a nasty occurrence in the near future. I needed to gather my troops for battle.

I took a deep breath. 'Aunt, I believe that my cousin, the one who has just left us, may be intending to propose imminently.'

'To whom, dear?' she asked mildly, not paying me much mind since she was eyeing the rest of the tart.

'To me! You must agree that he is not a suitable match!'

Aunt carefully cut herself another small slice of tart. 'You weren't keeping this, were you?' she asked Harriet, who shook her head.

'Aunt!' I was growing desperate.

She sighed. 'I don't entirely understand why you're so opposed to him, my dear. He seems like a kind and sensible young man. You could do a lot worse, Felicity.'

And with that, I deduced exactly what was going on. Papa knew of Mr Humbleton's intentions and approved since it meant protection for me. I would never have to fear being homeless if something happened to him.

Furthermore, I suspected that he'd told Aunt and had asked her to help smooth the way. That was why she'd hustled around here so quickly when she'd heard I was writing to Mr Fitzroy.

Doors started slamming up ahead in the hallway of my life.

All I needed now was for Harriet to join the throng, and my fate would be sealed: I'd be engaged to Mr Humbleton.

To me, it was a fate worse than death.

Chapter 10

Under normal circumstances, attending a ball at Ashbury Manor would have filled me with excitement. But when the day arrived and I took out my white muslin from the wardrobe and hung it up to air, all I felt was dread—dread that Mr Humbleton would cling like limpet to me all evening and not leave me alone. Or that I would have to anticipate his every movement to successfully avoid him. That reason, and that reason alone, was overshadowing any of the thrill I usually took in getting ready. I knew I wasn't going to have an enjoyable time of it.

'Perhaps I should stay at home,' I murmured, sitting on the bed and stroking the soft velvet brim of Mr Fitzroy's black hat.

'Pardon?' said Harriet from the dresser, where she'd been sorting through her jewellery box.

'I didn't say anything,' I replied.

'You did, and it sounded remarkably like you want to stay at home, which is an impossibility.'

'Do not mind me. Of course I am going.' *Even if I have to force myself ...*

She turned to face me, looking worried. 'Do you really think our cousin will propose to you? It seems outrageous that he would attempt it, especially as you've given him no encouragement whatsoever.'

'All indications point to it,' I said glumly.

'But surely, if he did, you could just say, "Thank you very much for the offer, but no thank you." Papa wouldn't scold you for that reply if he knew it would make you unhappy.'

'It depends how much Papa wishes to keep on the good side of my cousin. He holds a lot of power over us since he's the heir of our home.'

'Such a stupid little law,' grumbled Harriet. 'Whoever thought that up?'

'Some stupid little man,' I said flatly. We looked at each other and giggled, and I felt slightly better.

She held up a sapphire earring and a ruby earring next to each ear. 'Which do you think would go better with my dress?'

They were coloured glass, for we could only afford costume jewellery, but she was trying to secure a man who could give her the real thing.

'The ruby ones. They look more expensive,' I said.

'I have some seed pearls on a silk thread that would look lovely wound through your hair, if you want me to put it up for you?'

I could tell it was her attempt to encourage me; she wanted me to look forward to the ball tonight as much as she was. If I had a gentleman like Mr Pringle waiting for me there and who I knew wanted to dance every dance with me, then I too should be excited to attend. But I did not.

Harriet drew the pearls out of a black velvet bag to show me. I had to admit it was a pretty accessory.

'Where did you get it?'

'Aunt. She thought I might like it. She wore it on her wedding day.'

I cringed that I was about to wear a bridal adornment, yet here I was doing my best to avoid a marriage proposal from a man I didn't want to marry. But Harriet meant well.

I relented. 'All right. If I must.'

The carriage journey to Ashbury Manor was a repeat of how it had been the night of the supper: hot, squashed, and uncomfortable. Except that I was now dressed up in my finery and holding the blasted book to give to Mr Fitzroy.

How it would be received, I had no idea, and it was making me nervous. Harriet had given me the Gothic romance she'd been reading before we'd left as it was one she needed to return, and it fitted with my ruse.

'Tell him to return it to Mr Austen once he's finished

with it,' she'd said, adjusting her shawl.

'Oh, I don't think he'll actually read it …'

'Why not? You never know, he might have a penchant for Gothic romances. He looks the brooding type.'

So I clutched it in my sweating fist and avoided the gaze of Mr Humbleton, who was directly across from me. He'd attempted to speak to me before assisting me into the carriage (about what, I did not wish to know). But I'd successfully avoided the attempt by remarking upon the evening and looking up at the sky, which was studded with stars. 'What a lovely evening, is it not?'

The carriage hit a bump in the road, making us all yelp, and I gripped the book even tighter. Mr Fitzroy hadn't replied to my letter either. I hadn't expected him to as it had been very forward of me to write to him. But what if he'd considered it disgracefully impertinent and had ripped it to shreds? That would make the atmosphere between us even worse! With my anxiety spiking, plus the closeness and the swaying of the carriage, I started to feel slightly nauseous.

Finally, we pulled up outside Ashbury Manor amongst the other ball-goers' carriages and guests who were sorting out their finery as they alighted. Papa gave me his hand to step down. I looked up at the entranceway and spied Mr Pringle and Mr Fitzroy greeting guests one by one.

My stomach clenched with nerves. There was to be no

sidling in unnoticed. I was going to have to deliver the book to him in front of everyone. *Breathe*, I told myself. *He won't bite.*

But the firm set of his mouth when he glimpsed me amongst our party made me think otherwise. There was no welcoming smile from him, but Mr Pringle's beam when he saw Harriet made up for it ten times over.

'Miss Blackburn, how beautiful you look.' Upon grasping her gloved hand, he raised it to his lips and kissed it. I risked a look at Mr Fitzroy; his eyes were dark under his thickset brows, and his grim expression gave nothing away as he bowed silently to Harriet.

I gulped when it was my turn to stand in front of him.

'G-good evening, Mr Fitzroy,' I stuttered, bowing and feeling extremely ill at ease.

But he returned it smoothly. 'Miss Blackburn.'

'H-here is the book you wanted to read.' I thrust it at him, and he looked at it blankly. I could see he had no idea why I was giving it to him.

'You did get my letter, I hope?' I added, knowing that Aunt was next to me and listening to every word.

'Yes, I did, thank you.' He turned over the book and peered at the title. 'Is it a good ... read?'

'Gripping.' I replied. 'If you could please return it to Mr Austen when you have finished with it.'

There was an awkward silence as he tried to process what on earth I was talking about. I was relieved that he wasn't saying anything that would drop me in it; his taciturn nature was a boon in this circumstance.

But to my surprise, he spoke before I could move away. 'Miss Blackburn, would you do me the honour of standing up with me for the first dance?'

I felt like I'd dived into the lake and had duckweed in my ears. I almost said 'Pardon?' But I'd heard him as clear as a bell. He wished to dance with me.

'Yes,' I said faintly.

Harriet clutched at my arm and drew me, almost stumbling into the heat and noise of the candlelit ballroom. I, somewhat in shock and feeling like I needed smelling salts, leaned on her heavily.

'Let us proceed slowly around the room as if admiring it,' she whispered. 'It will give you time to calm yourself.'

I didn't think I would ever feel calm again. Our proceeding around the room and greeting people we knew went like this: walk, walk. Smile, nod.

'Did that just happen, or was it a dream?'

'Yes, dearest, it happened.'

Walk, walk. Smile, nod.

'Pray, did *Mr Fitzroy* just ask *me* to dance?'

'Yes, dearest, he did.'

Walk, walk. Smile, nod.

'So now I will actually dance with him?'

'Yes, dearest, you will.'

We rejoined our party on the opposite side of the room, and by that time, I had recovered my senses. It was just one dance; there was no harm in that, and it had neatly circumvented Mr Humbleton. That gentleman had excused himself the moment Harriet and I approached and took it upon himself to talk to a group of older women who were fluttering their fans. I breathed a sigh of relief and looked around for Jane but could not see her.

'Is Jane here?' I asked in general.

'Yes,' said Aunt. 'I caught sight of her arriving with her father and sister as we came in.'

Cassie had made it back in time for the ball. It was too bad that I was forbidden by Jane from pushing her into Mr Humbleton's arms!

Aunt turned sharp eyes towards me. 'I must say, I was surprised that Mr Fitzroy deigned to come down from his lofty perch to dance with you, a mere country girl. You must have said something to please him in that letter. Or perhaps it is only that he is grateful to you for bringing him his book.'

Aunt's comment brought me down to earth with a thump. Of course, he was simply being polite. To think he'd set his sights on me was a bit presumptuous on my part!

The strains of the orchestra tuning up for the first dance grew louder over the babble, and across the room, I saw Mr Pringle and Mr Fitzroy approaching in tandem towards us— one smiling widely and nodding to guests, the other doing his best not to smile or look at anyone if he could help it. The crowd seemed to part for them, being the most handsome and eligible gentlemen in the room, as they strode through.

'Here they come,' whispered Harriet. She, like me, seemed a little awestruck.

Mr Fitzroy's eyes locked on mine; and for a moment, the chatter ceased, and the room stilled.

Then they were in front of us. Mr Pringle whisked Harriet off without further ado, and Mr Fitzroy proffered his arm to me. 'Shall we?'

I took his arm gingerly, not daring to grasp it with too much force in case he bared his teeth. As he led me onto the floor, I couldn't help remarking, 'I'm surprised to see that you dance, Mr Fitzroy.'

'I think you'll find there are a lot of things about me that might surprise you, Miss Blackburn.'

Touché, I thought.

The music began, and we bowed to each other. I thought that this would be our lot for conversation. But Mr Fitzroy, for once, seemed inclined to talk.

'But a more pressing mystery, apart from your letter, which I was also wholly intrigued by', he continued, 'is why you have given me a Gothic romance novel.'

I flushed and averted my eyes as we went through the motions of the dance. Glancing at the sidelines as I sailed past, I happened to see Jane with her sister watching the dancers. Seeing me partnered with Mr Fitzroy, her mouth dropped open. She nudged Cassie, and they stared with interest. Goodness, was it that much of a strange thing for him to ask me to dance? But I too had been blindsided and had almost fainted when he did.

He was still waiting for my reply.

'Ah, it is a long and tedious story ... Not the novel, I assure you,' I added as I came back to him upon completing a turn. 'That, by all accounts, is wonderful, according to my sister.'

'I see I shan't be able to pry the mystery out of you.'

'It is quite harmless, rest assured,' I replied as we faced straight ahead. Our hands were lightly touching, which made it most difficult to concentrate on my steps.

'Well, thank you for letting me know my hat is safe and sound at least. I shall need to procure it from you.'

Is that why he asked me to dance, to get his hat back?

'Of course.'

'Perhaps I could call on you next week?'

He sounded genuine about this intention. Indeed, when we were facing each other again, I noted he looked rather nervous about my reply, if his darting eyes and tense jawline were anything to go by.

'So you accept my apology in good faith, about what happened at the pond?' I asked.

He nodded.

I let out a breath. Wonders would never cease. Not only had he forgiven me and asked me to dance, but now he wanted to call on me. Even though I knew it was mostly because he wanted to collect his hat, I was flattered.

'Very well. Shall we say Tuesday at three o'clock? If you are available?' I stated formally.

'Yes, that suits.'

Out of the corner of my eye, I saw Mr Humbleton hovering as we completed the finishing steps. Mr Fitzroy followed my gaze.

'Your cousin seems intent on asking you for the next dance.'

'He does,' I said tightly, my heart sinking.

'Perhaps I should dance with you for the entire evening so he cannot achieve his goal,' said Mr Fitzroy smoothly.

I gave him a small smile and said nothing, but a thrill shot through me. *What in heaven's name ...? Maybe it was not all about his hat!*

As we took our final bows, I noticed Jane, now alone, on the sidelines. She was peering intently at us, as if trying to work out what we were saying.

Harriet was dancing the next with Mr Pringle, and I had a wistful hope that Mr Fitzroy would make good on his statement and ask me to dance again. But he politely thanked me and melted away into the crowd. Maybe he had said it only in jest? I felt a bit lost after he'd left but came to my senses when I realised I was standing on the dance floor partnerless.

'Jane!' I hissed when I reached her side. 'We must talk!' I felt like I might burst if I didn't tell her, and Mr Humbleton had been distracted by another party of middle-aged ladies, so now was our chance.

'Come, let us find an alcove where we will not be disturbed,' she said in a serious tone, knowing that I must have something momentous to say after what she had just witnessed.

'Where is Cassie?'

'She's dancing the next. Do not worry. She is well informed about ... everything.'

Wondering exactly what Jane had been saying to Cassie, I followed her out of the ballroom.

We found a quiet corner in the room where supper was

being laid out, and I relayed to Jane in a hushed whisper behind my unfurled fan about what Mr Fitzroy had said— namely that he planned to call to retrieve his hat on Tuesday and that he'd noticed Mr Humbleton's interest in me and had seemed rather intent on securing me for all the dances.

'Tell me his exact words,' said Jane eagerly, unfurling her own fan to create more privacy.

'He said, "Perhaps I should dance with you for the entire evening so he cannot achieve his goal."'

Jane fluttered her fan excitedly. 'He likes you!' she whispered.

My cheeks blushed hotly as I remembered the way Mr Fitzroy had looked at me throughout the dance. My throat constricted, and I found it hard to swallow. 'I ... I had that same thought. But then I can't quite believe it either, especially after his piglet insult and our altercation at the lake.'

'A man can change his mind,' she said reasonably. 'I'm sure your letter of apology has gone some way to helping him take the blinkers off.'

'But I can't ... I *shouldn't* hope that he's calling for any reason other than his hat ...'

'Flissy, his hat is just an excuse. He's really calling to see *you*,' she said sagely as if she was privy to Mr Fitzroy's innermost thoughts, and I trusted her judgement. Jane had shown on many an occasion that she did have insight into the way upper-class gentlemen behaved when in pursuit of a woman (more insight than I had anyway!).

I fluttered my fan, feeling rather feverish all of a sudden as I realised I would not be averse to Mr Fitzroy calling to see me and for that purpose alone.

'Well then, if that is the case, I wonder what kind of cake he likes,' I pondered.

'Something solid and serious,' said Jane. 'Like pound cake.'

We giggled behind our fans.

There was the sound of someone clearing their throat, and we lowered our fans.

Mr Humbleton was standing there with a pompous look on his face. *Oh no*, I thought. *I was supposed to be keeping an eye out for him.*

'Ladies,' he said, bowing low. 'So sorry to disturb your conversation. I've come to invite my cousin to dance.'

I had the feeling he wasn't going to take no for an answer, so there was nothing for it but to agree or risk being extremely rude by scurrying away without a word and leaving Jane to make my apologies.

I pulled a face at her as he led me away, and she pouted in commiseration.

We'd been having fun after all until he'd shown up.

The experience of dancing with Mr Humbleton was nothing like that of dancing with Mr Fitzroy. I had to force myself to go through the motions. When he took my fingers, pressing them between his own limp cold ones, it was like holding hands with a mackerel. The thought of him touching any other part of my body made me shudder. But I had to go through with it for propriety's sake since he had asked me.

However, I could not help glancing surreptitiously about the room to discover the whereabouts of Mr Fitzroy— thinking, indeed, that he might ask me for the next dance and the next after that. Unfortunately, I wasn't paying much heed to my current dance partner; and soon, it was remarked upon.

'You seem distracted, cousin,' he said, inhaling sharply as I trod heavily on his foot for the second time.

'Do forgive me. I was looking for Harriet,' I muttered.

'She is dancing with Mr Pringle, further up the line.' He gestured with his head.

'Oh yes, I see now ...' I said, but words failed me when I clapped eyes on Mr Fitzroy dancing with an tall elegant lady with shining auburn hair. Her skin was translucent, and she wore diamond earrings and a matching necklace, which offset her gold-embroidered cream muslin dress.

She was beautiful, I couldn't deny it, even if her eyes

seemed a touch too large and her features a little too pointed. Most concerning, though, was that she seemed very attentive to Mr Fitzroy, peeping at him continuously through her lashes, though they were not making conversation as far as I could tell.

'Who is that woman?' I wondered aloud before I could stop myself.

'Lady Rosalind Whiteley,' supplied Mr Humbleton, attempting some fancy footwork to keep out of my way as I stepped forward when I was meant to be stepping back. 'She's a cousin of Mr Pringle's, I believe, who has come up from London specifically for the ball.'

Specifically for some other reason too perhaps, I thought, seeing her smile as Mr Fitzroy took her hand, and she twirled gracefully. A fierce stabbing pain overtook my entire chest when I saw him flick an approving glance at her. I whipped my head back to face the front, well aware that what I felt resembled pure, unadulterated jealousy.

Indeed, I fervently hoped that Lady Rosalind Whiteley would return to London immediately once the ball was over and not dally here in Steventon!

PART THREE

A Proposal

Chapter 11

'Oof, my feet are killing me. But the pain was worth it to spend time with him.' Harriet flopped onto our bed and kicked off her slippers. Tendrils of hair had come loose from her tight updo, and her muslin was slightly worse for wear. But her face was glowing, and I had never seen her look happier.

Harriet had danced almost every dance with Mr Pringle apart from one, when she'd pleaded for refreshment, and he'd raced off to the supper room. Upon his return, he'd supplied her with a goblet of lemonade and a plate of tasty morsels he'd hand-picked especially for her from the supper table. Then he'd taken her on a sedate tour of his library to provide a respite from dancing.

She'd told me all this in the carriage upon our return. We'd gone back home with Aunt after the dance, leaving Papa and Mr Humbleton to get a lift with a neighbour. Mr Pringle had invited them to stay on for longer and drink port and play cards with a few other gentlemen.

Aunt had given a disapproving tsk when she heard about the library tour. 'That was not appropriate. You and he left alone together in a room? I do wish you'd come and found me, Harriet. I would have gladly accompanied you.'

'There was a small party of us, Aunt, including Mr Fitzroy and Lady Whiteley. Besides, Evan is a gentleman. He always behaves with the utmost propriety.'

My heart had jumped at Mr Fitzroy's name ... but sank as soon as I'd heard that he had been accompanying that woman. I'd slumped back in the seat, the carriage wall bouncing against my spine, feeling exhausted from the onslaught of emotions I'd experienced throughout the evening: anticipation, surprise, excitement, wonderment, jealousy ... They were all there in varying forms and strengths from being subjected to that man.

Then there had been the vexation of dancing with my cousin and the energy I'd expended at having to avoid him thereafter. I was so busy keeping watch for him and flitting around the room that it was no wonder Mr Fitzroy hadn't made good on his promise to ask me for any more dances. However, that too may have been because Rosalind had sabotaged his company for the rest of the evening— something that made my blood boil every time I thought of it. Her looks, clothes, and jewels denoted her as very wealthy indeed; and it was making me extremely aware of my lower status. Even though Mr Fitzroy's glances and words denoted an attraction, surely, he wouldn't pursue me when there was a woman of higher class right in front of him? It depressed me wholly to think he might end up marrying her without me being considered in the slightest, especially now I had decided that I might quite like him to consider me. But I couldn't do anything about it. I just had to hope she'd take herself off back to London—alone.

'You were the belle of the ball,' I said to Harriet now, sitting on the other side of the bed and plastering a bright smile on my face. 'And the envy of every single woman there. It was plain to see he is captivated by you.'

She looked over at me, a dreamy smile playing across her lips. 'And I with him. Oh, Fliss, I cannot believe that he won't propose—it feels right ... in here.' She pressed a hand to her heart.

I nodded. 'Did he say anything that might suggest that he will?'

'No, but it can't be much longer, can it?'

'I'm sure that it won't be,' I said encouragingly.

Indeed, now that I had intended to live vicariously through Harriet's good fortune rather than bemoan my lack of it, I hoped Mr Pringle would go down on bended knee and as soon as humanly possible!

I had two more days of Mr Humbleton to put up with, and then I could reclaim my room—something I was looking forward to immensely. Although sharing with Harriet wasn't a burden, her continual happy humming was starting to grate on my nerves. And try as I might, I couldn't stop thinking about Mr Fitzroy and our one and only dance; the memory of how he'd looked at me and what he'd said was making me jittery. I wished I could be alone and muse about it and sort out my feelings, but I had to keep them to myself for the meantime. But would he still call on Tuesday afternoon to collect his hat? I had no clue.

Any time there was a knock on the front door, my heart fluttered, and my stomach leapt. But so far, there had been no letter of cancellation. I had to assume then that he was still calling. The thought filled me with light-headed anticipation. I couldn't for the life of me imagine what we would say to each other in a staid parlour setting.

On Monday afternoon, when Harriet and I were in that very same room, doing a little linen embroidery, time was running out; and I knew I had to tell her he was calling. But there didn't seem to be a right way to say it without causing undue fuss.

'Did he ... Did Mr Fitzroy say anything to you when you were in the library ... at the dance ... about calling this week?' I managed to get out in a fluster.

Harriet glanced at me curiously. 'He didn't. Did he say he would call on you?'

I tried to focus on my stitching, but it blurred before my

eyes. 'Ah, he said he might pop by on Tuesday at three o'clock to fetch his hat.'

She sat up straighter. 'Why did you not say so before?'

'It is just an errand,' I said. 'And of no consequence.'

'Exactly. Which is why he could have sent a servant to do it. But he has not.'

We stared at each other in silence. My heart thumped in my ears.

'Should I go and ask Sue to bake a cake then?' I asked slowly, laying my sewing aside.

'If you don't want him to eat dry biscuits with his tea, then you must!'

'Will you be here to play chaperone?'

She nodded. 'Of course. I wouldn't mention it to Aunt, though. Otherwise, word will have spread around the village before the day is out. Let us hope she doesn't decide to pop round when he calls.'

Feeling more confident about Mr Fitzroy's visit, I tripped off to the kitchen in search of Sue. I thought of what Jane had said about giving him pound cake, but it sounded much too dreary. No, surely, he'd find a light, but decadent sponge covered with jam and whipped cream much more memorable.

On Tuesday morning, I followed Harriet downstairs for breakfast with a lightness in my step. Mr Humbleton was leaving, and Mr Fitzroy was calling—it was going to be a joyous day!

We took our seats in the dining room as Mary finished laying out the various dishes. I decided to have a sizeable helping of scrambled eggs to fortify myself for the afternoon's event. Other ladies may have declined such a large breakfast, but I always became ravenous when I was nervous.

Mr Humbleton appeared and greeted us. I nodded to him and grabbed a roll in case he insisted on buttering one for me again. The sound of his carriage wheels disappearing down the road couldn't come fast enough in my opinion.

I planned to spend the rest of the morning transferring my belongings back to my room, throwing open the windows, and giving it a thorough airing to rid it of his scent. I hardly liked to sleep in my bed since he had lain in it, but I hoped clean linens would be enough of an exorcism (and maybe hanging several bunches of lavender around the room).

'Good morning, everyone,' said Papa upon entering and took his place at the top of the table.

'Morning, Papa!' Harriet and I chimed. Our cousin murmured his reply and kept peeling a boiled egg.

'You were up early this morning, Papa,' commented Harriet. 'I saw you strolling in the garden.'

'Yes.' He glanced at Mr Humbleton. 'I've had some things on my mind lately.'

Was it my imagination, or did Mr Humbleton's lips curl into a smug smile as he bit into his egg?

'Are you all packed for your journey, cousin?' I asked, determined to hurry him along. 'It may rain later, so you may want to leave directly after breakfast to avoid a muddy journey.'

Mr Humbleton gave me a tight smile, and his tongue moved under his top lip like an eel, extracting egg from his teeth before speaking; my toes curled in revulsion.

'I have not packed just yet. But I thank you for your concern about the roads, dear cousin. It is most thoughtful of you.'

I nodded and continued eating my breakfast in silence, trying to keep my jubilant mood intact, though I felt something like dread pressing upon me. *Please, God*, I begged silently, *just let him leave—and soon!*

But as long as he vacated before Mr Fitzroy's visit, there was no reason to be concerned. And the reorganising of my room could take place at any time. I could even spend another night in with Harriet and do it tomorrow.

I'd just finished my last mouthful of food and was leaning back, replete, when Mr Humbleton cleared his throat and announced, 'If I may, I would like a private audience with Miss Felicity.'

I sucked in my breath. *Oh noooo!* Whipping my head around, I tried to catch Papa's eye. But he was already dabbing his mouth with his napkin and rising, his breakfast half finished. 'Of course,' he said. So there was no help to be had there!

Harriet was also rising, but she at least had the grace to look as horrified as I felt.

'Please stay,' I mouthed.

She shook her head slightly.

'Harriet.' I made to grab her arm, but she was up and moving, following hot on Papa's heels. The dining room door slammed shut behind the two of them. I was alone, trapped by my cousin and bound by the laws of propriety that demanded I stay and listen to the dreaded speech that was about to come out of his mouth.

Staring fixedly at my egg-smeared plate, I sensed him leave his chair and come round to my side of the table. He made a gurgling noise to clear his throat, but I steadfastly refused to look at him.

There was a rustle of starched fabric as he sank to one knee.

Oh heavens above, I thought. *This refusal is going to be most excruciating, but he has brought it upon himself.*

'My dear cousin ... Miss Felicity,' he began. 'Throughout this fortnight of being in your company, I have become enamoured by your considerable charms ...'

I didn't speak a word.

He coughed and went on, 'I have deduced from staying in your bedroom that you and I would make an excellent match ...'

I could keep quiet no longer and pierced him with a glare. 'That's ridiculous! How on earth could you deduce that? Did the four walls tell you?' I scoffed. 'Cousin, you may have been staying in my room, but I was most decidedly not in it with you!'

'Pray, my apologies. Let me reword,' he said, sounding rattled, his ears bright red. I pressed my lips together in agitation. 'What I meant to say was, from my *vantage point* in your bedroom, I could see you set off on your daily walks. And I saw how you delighted in nature and all her esteemed bounties. This, I thought, was a lady who loved nature as much as I, and I rejoiced at finding a kindred spirit.'

So he'd been spying on me from my own bedroom window. I fought the urge to shudder violently.

'Sir—' I started, but he cut me off.

'So if you would do me the honour of being my wife, I would forever be indebted to you,' he finished in a hurry, undoubtedly wanting to wrap things up. 'Your father has given me permission to propose, and we have spoken at length about the entail. After much discussion, he came to the same conclusion as I—that it is to your great advantage if we marry.'

I closed my eyes, feeling betrayed. *Papa, how could you?*

There was no way this marriage would ever take place. I would rather throw myself off a cliff than marry Mr Humbleton.

He continued talking about where we would live, as if mentioning his 'small, but comfortable house in West Hertfordshire' would sway me to his line of reasoning—it did not. Then he switched to the wedding itself. 'I was thinking the end of March. The weather is warmer, and you could wear spring flowers in your—'

'Sir, you are too hasty. I have not given you an answer!' I cried. 'I am flattered at your proposing to me. But I do not love you, and I am convinced you do not love me in return. If I've given you any reason to believe that I have that kind of affection towards you, then I am sorry for it. But I do not. So unfortunately, I must decline your offer.' *Or fortunately, whichever way you wanted to look at it.*

Mr Humbleton didn't move from his bended-knee position. A fleeting look of panic crossed his face. I am not sure what he would have said next if Papa hadn't burst into the room, smiling from ear to ear and offering a hearty 'Congratulations!' Harriet trailed behind with wide eyes.

My cousin rose dazedly, only to have his hand pumped

enthusiastically by Papa.

'She has declined my offer,' he said stiffly.

There was an uncomfortable silence.

'Felicity, what is the meaning of this?' asked Papa in a low voice.

'It is simple, Papa. I do not want to marry him, and you cannot make me,' I said, folding my arms defiantly.

'I can, and I will. How dare you turn down your cousin's most generous proposal,' he said through gritted teeth. I glanced at Harriet, and I could see that Papa's demeanour had shocked her too. I'd never seen him look so angry. It cut me to the bone that he wasn't considering my feelings in the slightest. What had Mr Humbleton been blackmailing him with to get him to this point?

'I do not want to, Papa,' I repeated as steadily as I could.

'You. Will. Marry. Him,' he stated now, pointing a shaking finger at me.

'No, please! I can't, Papa!' I was starting to feel truly worried now.

Mr Humbleton bobbed up and down on his toes, looking from Papa to me like an anxious ferret. 'Sir, I can see that my proposal has been somewhat distressing for all concerned, something I had not planned for.' He gave Papa an accusing look to convey he should have better prepared me. 'I shall go for a walk to let things calm down a little, and perhaps you may help Miss Felicity to see reason.'

He made a short sharp bow to the room in general and swiftly left, closing the door softly behind him. Minutes later, I caught sight of his figure passing by the window, mopping his face with a handkerchief.

If he thought I could be talked into seeing reason, he could think again!

Papa sat down in the chair opposite me, his face drained and pale after his outburst. It was not like him to get so worked up.

'What has he been saying to you?' I demanded. 'There must have been something to cause such a reaction. I cannot seriously believe you would think I would marry a man I do not love.' I grasped his hands in mine. 'You know me, Papa! I could not!'

He sighed and glanced at the portrait of our mother on the wall. 'What one desires and what one gets in this life are two different things. I am sorry, Felicity, that it has come to this. He initially wanted Harriet, but I could not in good faith promise her to him because of Mr Pringle's singular attention that suggests he will indeed propose. It would be a most beneficial match for her.'

Harriet gave a gasp of pleasure, and I narrowed my eyes at her. A lucky escape!

'So I'm to be our cousin's unwilling victim simply because you do not have any more daughters to appease him with? Why can he not look elsewhere for a wife? Why do I have to be the sacrificial lamb?'

'He said it would be ... easier,' said Papa, averting his eyes.

I blinked. This couldn't be happening! I was to marry a man I couldn't stand because it was 'easier' for him?

I shook my head at him. 'This is outrageous!'

'I am truly sorry to put you in this position, but he is determined to leave here engaged.' He spread his hands helplessly. Mr Humbleton had so much power in this situation it was unbelievable, and he was taking full advantage of it.

'Is there perhaps another gentleman in the picture?' Papa enquired hopefully. 'If there was one that admired you to that extent, then I could see my way to putting him off. Is there such a man, my dear?'

Samuel crossed my mind fleetingly. If only I'd acted more enthusiastic about marrying him, I wouldn't be in this predicament. And even though he was calling on me in a few hours, I couldn't let myself entertain the notion that Mr Fitzroy felt even a smidgen of interest in that respect.

I shook my head despondently. 'There is not.'

'You could at least consider his offer, dearest,' Harriet said tentatively. She stepped behind Papa and rested a hand on his shoulder. 'Marrying our cousin will give you security for the rest of your life ...'

'But once you were married, I could live with you and Evan, could I not?' I said, staring at her.

'Of course you could. I believe, like Papa, that Evan's affection is such that he will propose. Yet what if something happens to him before he does? He might fall off his horse or have a carriage accident ... However unlikely, we have to think of that. So your match with Mr Humbleton would protect me too.'

Anger bubbled up in me at her siding with Papa. To me, it looked like the two of them were in cahoots!

'Then you marry him! He wanted you first after all!' I cried.

'Fliss, Papa has your best intentions at heart ...'

By this, time tears were falling down my cheeks in fast succession.

'But I don't love him!' I wailed. 'I can't even stand talking to him, let alone him touching me!'

A vision of Mr Humbleton attempting to climb on top of me on our wedding night made me shudder violently.

And once I'd started shuddering, I couldn't stop.

Chapter 12

Mr Humbleton told Papa that he'd decided to extend his stay for another week. Apparently, no matter how devoted he was to the goodly souls of his parish, securing a wife before he returned was now top priority.

However, he was smart enough to lie low for the rest of the morning, and he did not appear for luncheon. Was he hoping for Papa and Harriet to wear me down so that I would give in? I couldn't understand why he would want to marry me when I so vehemently despised him. Was he of the opinion that love could grow where hate currently festered? I couldn't make him out at all.

With all this going on, the time for Mr Fitzroy to call grew near, and I felt like my brain was going to explode. How could I sit and make polite conversation when I was still so angry with Papa and Harriet? I couldn't have suggested a worse time for him to visit.

But there was nothing for it but to sit in the parlour with Mr Fitzroy's velvet brimmed hat in my lap and wait. Harriet sat across from me, concentrating on her needlework, not speaking. I couldn't bear it. We needed to be on better terms. Otherwise, the meeting would be even more unspeakably awkward than I envisioned it being.

In desperation, I plopped his hat on my head.

'Harriet!' I growled. 'Look at me, I'm Mr Fitzroy.' I scowled and attempted to mimic his gruff expression.

Her lips twitched. 'Fliss, stop it. He'll be here any minute.'

Encouraged, I strode across the room to the mantelpiece and stood there, gazing haughtily at her. 'I never dance if I can help it,' I said loudly in a gravelly voice. 'Unless my partner is well known to me, and even then, I may still refuse to.'

Harriet chortled. 'Oh, you sound just like him!'

There was a soft knock at the door. 'A gentleman for Miss Felicity,' said Mary, bobbing. Before I could do anything, Mr Fitzroy had appeared in the doorway, and I was caught. He stood stock-still, scanning the scene before him, and I could tell by the frown on his face that he had heard what I'd said from the hallway and that he didn't approve of my impersonation.

Most embarrassed, I quickly rearranged my features and tossed his hat onto the sofa. His frown deepened, no doubt at my lack of concern for his personal belongings.

Harriet stood and went forward to greet him calmly as if nothing was amiss.

'Mr Fitzroy, how nice of you to visit. Do come in! We were listening for your carriage or a horse, but we heard none. Did you walk over from Ashbury?'

'I did,' he said. 'The weather was so nice today I took it upon myself to get some fresh air. I find walking to be even more pleasant when you have a visit with friends at the other end of it.'

He glowered at me, and I felt awful that he had been looking forward to this outing and I had ruined it with my silly play-acting.

'Indeed it is,' I said, knowing I needed to make amends. 'Please, won't you sit down? Mary will bring in tea shortly. And I asked our cook to make a cake especially as I knew you were coming.'

Mr Fitzroy nodded, his forehead smoothing, and I breathed a sigh of relief. For a moment there, I had thought he might snatch up his hat and stalk out the door, vowing never to speak to me again.

He lowered himself to the sofa, moving his hat out of the way first, while I sat in the chair opposite.

'I trust Evan ... Mr Pringle ... is well?' enquired Harriet, picking at a loose thread in her embroidery.

'He is,' replied Mr Fitzroy. 'From what I have seen of him. His cousin Lady Whiteley has been keeping him occupied of late, visiting some relations of theirs in the area.'

'Oh how lovely!' said Harriet. 'It was unfortunate that we were not introduced to her at the ball.'

Mr Fitzroy clicked his tongue. 'I shall remedy that and let her know you would like to make her acquaintance. No doubt she will invite you both to tea. It is one of her favourite pastimes.'

I resisted the urge to wrinkle my nose in displeasure. Taking tea with Rosalind Whiteley wasn't something I particularly wanted to do. But Harriet seemed well disposed to the notion because she said, 'Oh yes, please do. I would like that!'

'How long does she plan to stay at Ashbury?' I asked, being careful to keep my voice neutral and not give any hint of jealousy.

'I am not sure,' said Mr Fitzroy, matching my tone. 'I am not privy to her diary.'

He gave me a glance that I couldn't quite read, but it was as if he knew what I was really asking: *How is it between you? And are you attached to her in any way, shape, or form?*

My eyes lingered on his, and a tendril of something grew between us—a feeling that tugged in my chest and made me want to ask him all manner of questions that were quite unsuitable.

But I clenched my hands in my lap and forced myself to

look away. Mr Fitzroy, in his fine suit and neatly tied cravat, was altogether too handsome; and it was difficult not to feel overwhelmed by his presence at such close quarters. It was astounding, really, that he was sitting here in our humble parlour when I knew he was used to much grander surroundings.

The door to the parlour swung open. 'Here's Mary with the tea,' I began in relief. But before I could finish my sentence, Mr Humbleton strolled in and let out an exclamation of surprise when he saw that the room contained our small party.

'Oh, do forgive me! I didn't realise we were having company. Good day, Mr Fitzroy.' He gave a low bow, which Mr Fitzroy returned with a nod.

'To what do we owe this pleasure?' said our cousin, plopping into the nearest armchair and crossing his legs.

'I was just retrieving my hat from Miss Felicity.' Mr Fitzroy gestured to the accessory, now resting on the arm of the sofa.

'Your hat?' said Mr Humbleton, looking confused. 'Pray tell, how did Miss Felicity come to be in possession of it?'

Mr Fitzroy's eyes met mine again, but this time, more intently. Heat rose in my face as I remembered him emerging from the pond, his wet shirt not leaving much to the imagination.

'I ... I found it in a field last week,' I said, not knowing how to continue with that line of reasoning. But Mr Fitzroy came readily to my aid.

'Yes, she did,' he stated smoothly. 'And she kindly conveyed as such to me at the ball. I'd been out riding, you see, and only realised I was without my hat when I returned to Ashbury.'

I stared at him, a little taken aback at the complexity of his fib. But it seemed he was just as anxious as I to conceal the true interaction that had taken place between us, no doubt in case my clergyman cousin deemed it unholy!

'But how did she know it was yours? That is remarkable powers of deduction, even for my dear cousin, whose intelligence I esteem greatly.' He smirked at me.

I felt like scoffing; 'esteem greatly?' What poppycock!

'Not so remarkable,' I returned curtly. 'We met by chance one day in Overton, and he was wearing it then. I took notice of it since it suited him so well ...'

Mr Fitzroy's lips curled into a smile, and I realised I'd unwittingly paid him a compliment. He inclined his head to me, and Mr Humbleton looked displeased.

'So that is the story of the hat! Where is Mary with that tea and cake?' I said, desperate to change the subject.

'I'll go and find out,' said Harriet hastily. Now that Mr Humbleton had joined us, she could leave the room; before, it would have been impossible as Mr Fitzroy and I would have been left alone together.

'Here we are!' announced Harriet a moment later. She re-entered the room carrying a serving plate upon which was perched a gigantic sponge cake; jam oozed down its sides, and the top was covered liberally with swirls of cream. Mary followed behind with a tray of tea-things.

'I hope you like sponge cake,' I said to Mr Fitzroy, noticing he had raised an eyebrow at the size of it. 'I'm sure I told our cook we were having one guest, not twenty.'

His mouth quirked. 'I do indeed. Might I trouble you for a generous slice? After all, I need fortification for my return journey.'

Feeling pleased that I'd made the right decision on the type of cake that he liked, as soon as Harriet set it down on the sideboard, I jumped up and did the honours. Plunging the knife into the heart of it, I cut Mr Fitzroy a man-sized piece and hefted it onto a china plate.

I was about to hand it to him when Mr Humbleton, who was sitting in proximity, cleared his throat in that annoying guttural way he had.

'Cousin, I do believe you should give me the first slice.'

I swivelled. 'Pardon?'

He gestured to the cake plate I held, which was hovering in front of him. 'It is an old-fashioned formality to be sure, but one that is still generally accepted—the gentleman of the house should be served first.'

I narrowed my eyes. I had never heard of such a formality, which meant there was a strong chance he was fibbing.

'I do not know what you are talking about.'

He grasped the edge of the plate and tugged it towards him.

'It is well known and practised where I come from,' he insisted.

I tugged it back, feeling annoyed. 'We are not in West Hertfordshire now, sir. Kindly unhand the plate.'

Harriet was looking between the two of us nervously but decided not to intervene.

'It is also common courtesy', he continued glibly, 'since I am your intended ... husband.'

I sensed, rather than saw, Mr Fitzroy start in surprise at this information.

'Let. It. Go!' I hissed. With an almighty tug, I wrenched the plate out of Mr Humbleton's clammy hand. But the cake, although dense, was not sufficiently anchored to it; and it flew in an arc, over my shoulder, and landed neatly in Mr Fitzroy's lap, splattering cream, and jam all over his black silk trousers.

'Oh no!' cried Harriet, sounding distressed.

With a fierce glare at Mr Humbleton, I took up a napkin and went over to assist Mr Fitzroy, who was gazing fixedly at the slice of cake in his lap.

'I am so very sorry,' I said quietly, holding the plate level with his thigh. 'If you would allow me ...' With my hand, I levered the cake off his lap and onto the plate in one swift motion but saw, with dismay, it had left behind a mess.

Using the napkin, I attempted to wipe the cream off his lap, but there was a lot of it. As I gently patted here and dabbed there, I could not help but notice Mr Fitzroy had begun breathing quite erratically. He suddenly grasped my wrist with his large warm hand and murmured, 'Miss Blackburn, please do not concern yourself.'

'But ...' I stared at the greasy stain, feeling terrible.

'Should I fetch a jug of water and some soap?' Harriet called over.

'Thank you, but no, I do not think it will help,' said Mr Fitzroy. He let go of my wrist and stood abruptly, brushing off the remaining crumbs that clung, while I hovered with the napkin, wondering if I should attempt to dab at his lap again. He seemed wholly intent not to let me near it.

Mr Humbleton, meanwhile, had proceeded to cut himself a large slice of cake and was now forking it into his mouth in a self-satisfied manner.

'If you need some new trousers, Mr Fitzroy, I'm sure Mr Blackburn would be delighted to assist,' he said with a chuckle.

'There is no need. I shall ask our housekeeper to attend to these forthwith.' Mr Fitzroy collected his hat, and I saw that he meant to take his leave.

'Oh, you don't have to go,' I said quickly.

'I feel I must, for the sake of my trousers,' he said with a half smile that didn't quite reach his eyes. He bowed to me. 'Good day, Miss Blackburn. I will leave you to your sister and your ... fiancé.'

He nodded to Harriet and Mr Humbleton, then strode swiftly to the door and was out of the room before I could stop him. I let out a small cry of anguish, for there was more than just damaged trousers at stake.

I hated Mr Humbleton at that moment. He'd managed to ruin a lovely tea party and a blossoming ... friendship ... and he hadn't even been invited.

I rounded on him, a blaze of anger surging through me. 'How dare you say you are my intended husband in front of Mr Fitzroy!' I said tightly. 'You are *not*, and I trust you never will be. I could never marry a man *I despise so immensely!*'

Not waiting for a response, I ran out of the room, hoping to catch up to Mr Fitzroy and rectify matters—namely tell him in not so many words that I was still a single lady and very much unattached!

Though I was fond of walking and deemed myself of a hardy constitution, Mr Fitzroy had longer legs than I and was striding so hurriedly that he was halfway across the field by the time I'd even reached the first stile. Nevertheless, I determinedly gave chase, lifting up my skirt and dodging cowpats, such was the urgency in me to convey the truth. If he should go to sleep tonight thinking I was engaged to that man, then it was almost as if my fate would be sealed (at least in his mind). I had to put him right.

But I was not wearing my walking boots. I was in thin-soled slippers more suited to a ballroom than an uneven ground with rough clods of earth and divots from horses and cows. Suffice to say, I tripped over several times, managing to right myself on each occurrence but was not so lucky on the last, when I stepped into a hole and went over on my ankle, falling heavily. I cried out and held it tightly for some moments to quench the pain. When it had lessened a little, gingerly, I stood and tested it with a single step. Although sore, it was not debilitating, and I continued (albeit limping) after the impervious figure who was now far ahead and drawing farther away from me.

'Mr Fitzroy! Stop!' I shouted to him. But his top hat disappeared over the brow of a hillock and vanished from sight.

I let out a cry of frustration.

Then it began to rain, a miserable downpour that soon wet me through.

At this time, I was closer to Jane's house than my own. So I veered towards it and limped along as best as I could, leaning against trees and fence posts to rest. My ankle by now was truly painful and swelling fast. If only Mr Fitzroy had deigned to look back, I was sure he would have come to my rescue, even carried me in his strong arms to Ashbury. It was a romantic fancy indeed! And one that was comforting enough to keep me hobbling onwards through the mud.

It was in this heightened state of emotion that I pounded on the Austens' front door. Amy took one look at my bedraggled, sodden appearance and quickly ushered me in out of the rain, where I proceeded to leave a large puddle on their flagstone entranceway.

'Come through to the kitchen, miss, where it's warm.'

I stepped forward and almost buckled from the pain shooting up my leg. 'I'm sorry, I can't. My ankle,' I gasped. Now that the happy vision of Mr Fitzroy carrying me had vanished into thin air, I could no longer walk.

Amy put her strong arm around my waist, and I leaned upon her shoulder heavily and made slow wincing progress to the kitchen, where the stove was emanating a comforting warmth.

She pulled out a chair for me and another to prop up my ankle. 'I'll fetch Miss Jane. She'll know what to do.'

That makes sense, I thought wearily. Jane was a stoic defender for the weak and injured. Whenever the animals of the Austen menagerie were ill, she always wanted to nurse them back to health, whereas her mother was more likely to put them to sleep to save the bother.

There was the sound of slippered feet running, and Jane burst into the room.

'Flissy, what on earth has happened? Your hair!'

Wonderingly, I touched my hair, discovering it had come loose from its carefully pinned chignon and was hanging like rat's tails on either side of my face and dripping down my back.

I opened my mouth, but my throat constricted, and no words came out. Where should I even begin to explain the day I was having?

I shook my head at her. 'Don't try to speak if you don't want to,' she said kindly, and tears welled in my eyes.

'Amy said you had hurt your ankle?'

I nodded mutely and pointed to my left foot, currently propped on the chair. She removed my slipper and gently pressed around my stockinged ankle with her fingers, then moved it to the left and to the right, and I let out a gasp. 'Is that sore?'

'A little,' I croaked.

'I do not think it is broken, perhaps just a nasty sprain.' Straightening up, she sprang into practical mode. 'Amy, please could you fetch a towel, a bowl of warm water, and a bandage.'

After washing my ankle and binding it tightly, Jane dried off my hair and cleaned smudges of dirt off my face. As she helped me climb the stairs to her and Cassie's parlour, she talked reassuringly all the while, saying that I needn't worry and that I could stay with them for the night and that she'd asked Amy to look out one of Cassie's dresses for me since she was more my size and that I would be dry and warm in no time.

As we made our way up, step by agonising step, my distress about Mr Fitzroy not turning around when I had fallen morphed into the feeling of utmost relief. Imagine if he had carried me to Ashbury? Turning up in this state with Rosalind staying there would have been mortifying. I doubted she would have wiped the dirt off my face, wrapped my ankle, or loaned me one of her fine dresses. No, I was in the best place possible—with my dear friend Jane, who would look after me.

Chapter 13

Jane and Cassie fussed around after me like a couple of mother hens. Soon, I was in dry clothing, lying on their sofa with my injured ankle propped on a cushion, along with a cup of tea in my hand and a nourishing plate of tidbits at my elbow should I feel hungry. I felt like a princess. As the weather worsened outside, again, I congratulated myself on coming here rather than returning home.

'I have sent word to Harriet via our stable boy that you have hurt your ankle and are staying here for the night to rest it,' said Jane, indicating that I should lean forward so she could place another cushion behind my shoulders. 'You should keep off it as much as possible in the coming days too.'

'I agree,' said Cassie, turning to look at me from where she was kneeling by the grate and attempting to coax a fire to life with a pair of bellows. 'I twisted my ankle very badly once, but I was impatient and insisted on walking on it. It took much longer to heal. Father fetched the doctor, and he said I was not to walk on it for another two weeks! I was bored out of my mind.'

'She was,' commented Jane. 'And she made a terrible patient.'

Cassie grinned. The log in the grate caught, and as the flames started to crackle, I noted in the firelight that she was looking refreshed and rested after her stay in Kent. Her face bloomed with health, and she'd caught a slight tan on her arms.

I sipped my tea and enquired, 'How do you like being back, Cassie?'

She perched on a nearby chair and considered the question. Three years older than Jane, Cassandra was her constant companion and touchstone; the two were very close—closer than even Harriet and I. A fresh wave of pain arose in me, thinking about Harriet and her siding with Papa, so I tried not to.

'I missed everyone, of course, but Jane kept up a steady supply of correspondence and painted me a vivid picture of the goings-on. I especially enjoyed the supper at Ashbury Manor, a delightful scene. Your cousin sounds like a most entertaining fellow.' She gave a little laugh.

I looked at Jane, wondering exactly what she had said about Mr Humbleton and in what context. But I trusted Cassie, and I knew she wouldn't spread gossip. Otherwise, Jane would not be so free with her opinions and descriptions; she was highly creative after all, and Mr

Humbleton had been entertaining, even if now he was causing me chronic consternation.

I had still not given Jane a reply as to why I had turned up wet and distressed on her doorstep, and I knew she must be burning with curiosity. Heaving a sigh, I stared intently at my empty teacup; it was probably best that I said it directly without any embellishment.

'Speaking of my cousin, he has asked me to marry him. The proposal was made at breakfast this morning.'

There was a shocked silence.

'Oh, my dear,' murmured Jane, knowing that this was the last thing I wanted to occur. 'What did you say?'

'I turned him down—politely, of course,' I stated. 'But he is refusing to take no for an answer. And ... and Papa and Harriet seem to think I should accept.' My voice wobbled, and I glanced up at the ceiling and took a breath to calm myself before continuing.

'The whole thing is outrageous. Don't you think so? I cannot marry a man I don't love—and one that I, in fact, am beginning to hate!'

Jane sat on the edge of the sofa and took my hand. 'Of course you should not be expected to marry him,' she said in a matter-of-fact tone.

'Hear! Hear!' said Cassie. 'It's 1796, not 1596. We get so few freedoms as it is. A woman should at least have some say about who she marries, even if she can't own the house she lives in.'

'Well, actually, that is the crux of the matter,' I said sadly. 'Our house is entailed to him. So if we marry, I would have security for the rest of my life. And Harriet too. If I do not and something happened to Papa, Mr Humbleton would have every right to toss us into the street. So it is almost my duty—'

'We would take you in,' interrupted Jane confidently. 'I've always wanted more sisters.'

'Oh ...' Hope rose in me but then fell. 'Your parents would never agree to it. They have so many children as it is.'

'Yes, but several have moved out, so there is space.'

It was a kind thought, but I still didn't think her father would appreciate two more mouths to feed.

'Is he so disagreeable, your cousin?' asked Cassie curiously.

I nodded. 'He is smarmy and pompous and talks about nothing of consequence.' I opened and closed my hand like it was a duck's bill. 'And we have nothing in common.'

'Except perhaps stubbornness,' said Jane with a smile. 'He seems determined to have you.'

'But why? It is almost out of spite, as if he is trying to bend my will, like I am a challenge to him!'

A vision of myself walking down the aisle and Mr

Humbleton waiting at the other end wearing a triumphant smile floated across my mind. It seemed entirely plausible that he might win.

'Jane, what am I going to do?' I asked anxiously. 'I can't marry him. If I do, I'm lost to society a-and anyone else who I might actually want to marry. And there is no way I could bear a child to him ... The thought of him touching me ...'

My fear of being pregnant after what had happened to my mother was bad enough, but being pregnant by him would be ten times worse!

Jane patted my hand. 'Do not fret. You will just have to stay strong and keep saying no and that you will only marry for true love! Hopefully, your father will come to his senses and not enforce it in some way.'

She got up and stood in front of the fire, looking thoughtful. 'What about if I recite a few of Shakespeare's sonnets to him? So he can appreciate that a woman must marry for love?' Clasping her hands together in front of her bosom, she lifted her chin and quoted,

Let me not to the marriage of true minds
Admit impediments; love is not love
Which alters when it alteration finds,
Or bends with the remover to remove.
O no, it is an ever-fixèd mark
That looks on tempests and is never shaken ...

Cassie and I clapped, and Jane bowed, her cheeks flushing. 'I would not hesitate if I thought it would help,' she said solemnly, and I stifled a giggle, imagining her forcing Papa to listen to her quoting Shakespeare on my behalf.

'It was very rousing,' I said. 'Thank you.'

It was kind of her to try to comfort me and cheer me up. I felt as if Jane and Cassie were at least on my side, which was more than I could say for Harriet, my own sister!

'But what about Mr Fitzroy? Wasn't he calling today?' asked Jane.

I stared into the fire and mumbled, 'Zounds, that was even worse.'

'What happened?'

I sighed and twisted my fingers together in my lap. 'I suppose I should start from the beginning.'

Recounting Mr Fitzroy's visit brought it back to painful life, but Jane and Cassie seemed enthralled as I explained how he'd had first caught me impersonating him, and then things had gotten progressively worse. 'I was about to serve him a slice of sponge, but Mr Humbleton insisted on having it. There was a tug of war with the plate. Then unfortunately, the cake went flying and landed in Mr Fitzroy's lap!'

'Oh, that's excellent!' Jane crowed.

I stared in amazement at her sparkling eyes and face creased with merriment.

'No, it was a nightmare, Jane! He had cream and jam all over his trousers, and the more I tried to wipe it off, the worse it became ...' I swallowed, remembering him murmuring to me and grasping my wrist. 'H-he felt an urgent need to leave in haste!'

Jane, by this time, was in fits and clutching her stomach. 'Oh stop, Flissy, don't say any more. It hurts ...' she gasped.

Cassie was also trying not to laugh, and I finally permitted myself to see the humour of it. My mouth quirked. 'He said the housekeeper would tend to his trousers, but I am not entirely sure how he would explain it ... The stain on his crotch was ... sizeable.'

Tears rolled down Jane's face. 'Oh my goodness, that's the funniest thing I ever heard.' She hiccupped and wiped her eyes with the sleeve of her dress.

'You can tell no one, either of you! Do you swear on your lives?'

Jane and Cassie nodded in tandem, then fell about giggling madly again. I joined them, my spirits magically improved by the medicine of laughter.

When we'd all calmed down, I supplied the last bit of the story—that Mr Humbleton had told Mr Fitzroy that he was my intended husband.

'Which was a blatant lie! I never said yes to him! And he calls himself a Christian.' I folded my arms grumpily.

'Or he's just extremely hopeful,' said Jane. I snorted.

'I ran out to try to catch up to Mr Fitzroy to set him straight, but he was too far ahead, and I wasn't wearing suitable footwear. Then it started raining, and well ...' I gestured to my ankle. 'You know the rest.'

'Do you think he left in a hurry because of the state of his trousers or Mr Humbleton's news?' asked Cassie.

'I have no idea.' I tried to recall the timing of things. 'He seemed to react unfavourably when he heard him say it, but then the cake incident occurred, and he may have used that as an excuse to leave. Suffice to say, I doubt he will be calling again.'

'And that isn't what you wanted, is it, dear?' asked Jane, looking at me quizzically, and I felt like she was gently assessing my heart like she'd done my ankle.

Tears pricked at my eyes, and I looked away, unwilling to comment.

However, the subject of Mr Fitzroy's visit was quickly dropped as Mrs Austin bustled in to see how I was faring; and my ankle was unbound, examined, and commented on, then bound again.

It wasn't until later on that evening when Cassie and Jane had retired to their room and I was lying on my makeshift sofa bed that I started to sift through my feelings. There was no longer any doubt in my mind that I was in some danger of liking Mr Fitzroy too much for my own good despite his higher status and the complexity that entailed. His face was ever fascinating to me and rather like a cloud-filled sky on a winter's day. Just today, I had witnessed it dark and brooding, then momentarily clearing with a brief respite from the rain (perhaps even a peep of sun). Then when the chill wind had blown, it reverted again to thick and impenetrable cloud.

What he thought of me, I couldn't fathom. But I sensed I held some sway over his mind, that he was drawn to me inexplicably (even if I was a kind of curiosity) and that Mr Humbleton's ill-timed comment had pierced his armour.

Closing my eyes, I played out the scene as it should have gone. Mr Fitzroy not striding away across the field but leaning against the oak tree, staring at the house and looking morose. His scowl would lift a little when I came running up to him, panting, and I would have said something like 'Sir, why did you leave in such a hurry? I was going to cut you another slice of cake.'

His expression would darken inexorably.

'I could not stay after hearing that you are to be married. And to that man? I cannot take pleasure in news such as that. It was disgusting. I had to leave before I said something I would no doubt regret.'

I, of course, would be taken aback by his strength of feeling but also curious as to what he would have said and have edged a little closer.

'Why not say it now? There is no one here but us.'

I pictured his cheeks pinkening slightly and his breathing quickening as I approached to stand before him.

'I cannot. I ...'

'Maybe we don't need words,' I would say sultrily, placing a finger on his quivering lips.

He would be silent but look at me intensely as I caressed the side of his face and placed my hand on his strong chest and felt the heat emanating from him. Then he would be so overcome with need that he would have to kiss me, fervently ...

The kissing scene was so vivid and pleasing to me that I became quite overcome with a paroxysm of desire and gripped the edge of the small table at the side of the sofa for support.

Unfortunately, it wobbled precariously, causing Jane's writing slope to tip open, her quill to drop out, and a couple of her papers to flutter to the floor.

Muttering a silent curse, I set about fixing the desk to rights, keeping an eye on the bedroom door. But there were no footsteps or drowsy voices enquiring what on earth I was doing out here. I breathed again. Thank goodness they were soundly asleep! Reaching down to collect the papers, which were covered in Jane's elegant cursive, I glanced at a page briefly before I went to put them back in the desk. But something caught my eye, which made me peruse it more closely. I had assumed she was writing a letter, but it appeared to be more like dialogue.

'What is his name?'

'Bingley.'

'Is he married or single?'

'Oh! Single, my dear, to be sure! A single man of large fortune; four or five thousand a year. What a fine thing for our girls!'

And so it went on, a conversation between a man and his wife (a woman who I instantly disliked) about some young man who had let a house called Netherfield. What was this? Something that she'd overheard in the village? I knew most of the families in Steventon, and none of them had a single rich son who was called Bingley. If there had been, his presence wouldn't have remained hidden for long! I looked further down the page, where another couple of random paragraphs had been written.

What a contrast between him and his friend! Mr Darcy danced only one dance with Mrs. Hurst and once with Miss Bingley, declined being introduced to any other lady, and spent the evening in walking about the room, speaking occasionally to one of his own party. His character was decided. He was the proudest, most disagreeable man in the world, and everybody hoped he would never come there again.

A slow realisation came over me, and I let out a soft chuckle. These weren't real people that she was writing about. Well, they were based on real people, and two of them I knew. Eagerly, I scanned down the page.

'She is tolerable but not handsome enough to tempt me; I am in no humour at present to give consequence to young ladies who are slighted by other men. You had better return to your partner and enjoy her smiles, for you are wasting your time with me.'

Mr Bingley followed his advice. Mr Darcy walked off; and Elizabeth remained with no very cordial feeling towards him. She told the story, however, with great spirit among her friends; for she had a lively, playful disposition, which delighted in anything ridiculous.

My hand flew to my mouth, and I stifled a giggle. *Jane! How utterly delicious. And so naughty!*

Hastily, I poked her quill and papers safely back into the writing slope, feeling like I had read her personal diary. The subject was a little close for comfort, but if it pleased her to write it, who was I to scold when I was so obviously Elizabeth and she'd painted me in a good light? Mr Darcy did not fare as well!

Admittedly, I felt slightly discomforted, but, at the same time, flattered to be thought interesting enough for her to write about, even in random scribblings. As long as her papers remained in this room and were never read by the real Mr Bingley and Mr Darcy, then I did not think they would cause any real harm.

Chapter 14

Despite Jane and Cassie doing everything to make me as comfortable as possible on the sofa, I had a fitful night, tossing and turning—at once too hot and flinging the blanket off, then shivering with cold and unable to get warm. My ankle throbbed relentlessly, a persistent reminder of Mr Fitzroy and his disastrous visit.

I fell asleep in the early hours of the morning, exhausted, only to be plunged into an intense dream where I was running and calling after a gentleman dressed in black. It was to no avail, and he disappeared into a thick fog. Then I looked down, and I was thigh-deep in mud. 'It's no use trying to run,' said a voice. 'You're stuck well and good.' Slowly, I turned and saw Mr Humbleton with a self-satisfied look on his face. He was dressed in nothing but a white shirt, which he started to unbutton ...

I woke in a fright, my armpits sweaty and my throat dry. But although I told myself it was just a dream, it took some time for my heart to calm and stop thudding against my breastbone. I didn't attempt to sleep again.

When dawn broke, Jane came tiptoeing into the parlour,

yawning. She was still in her nightgown with a red shawl wrapped around her shoulders.

'Good morning!' she sang cheerfully upon seeing I was awake.

'Morning,' I replied listlessly. Her eyes flicked over me, but she didn't press me for details of how I'd slept as it was obvious my answer would be 'not well'. She silently wet a cloth from a basin of water, wrung it out, and passed it to me so I could wipe my face and neck.

'After breakfast, I will ready the carriage to take you home,' she said.

I sighed inwardly. Part of me was hoping I could stay at the Austens' for the rest of the week and avoid having to cope with Mr Humbleton, but it was not reasonable to expect that.

Just as I'd finished dressing, with Jane supporting me with her arm, there was a knock at the door. 'Come in!' Jane called out, thinking it was Amy. But Harriet walked into the room, her expression grave. She was wearing her dark-blue riding dress with a matching hat and gloves.

'Oh, hello! What are you doing here?' I asked in surprise.

'Papa sent me in the buggy to collect you. However, I had a lot of trouble with George. He wouldn't obey me. He's as stubborn as a mule. He only listens to you.'

I stifled a grin. Good old George.

'He does, but barely,' I said. 'All right, I'll drive on the way home. I don't need my ankle for that.'

She nodded and remembered her manners. 'Hello, Jane. Thank you so much for looking after Fliss.'

'It was no trouble at all. Would you care for a cup of tea or ...?'

Harriet shook her head. 'Thank you, but we should be on our way.'

We proceeded slowly down the stairs and outside, with Harriet and Jane supporting me and Cassie hovering. My ankle felt better than it did yesterday, but it was still too tender to put my entire weight on it.

'Write to me and let me know how it goes with Mr You-Know-Who,' Jane whispered as Harriet was untying George's reins.

I wasn't sure if she meant Mr Humbleton or Mr Fitzroy, but either way, I now knew after reading her scribblings that she was eager for more anecdotes to further her story.

'Of course,' I said, hugging her. 'You will be the first to hear.'

George was a right royal pain on the journey back, and it took all my powers of concentration to keep him moving along the road. I was tempted to use the whip on him, but from experience, it usually made him play up more.

'He is worse than usual,' I said. 'When my ankle has healed, I'll take him for a ride. He has been cooped up too long in the stable.'

Harriet didn't reply, and I glanced at her. She was sitting ramrod straight, staring fixedly into the distance. 'I have made up my mind. I will marry him,' she murmured.

'There's no need to go to that extreme,' I scoffed. 'I'm sure we can find him a willing mare.'

'Not George—our cousin!'

I stared at her in shock. 'What?'

Her lips pursed. 'I will marry Mr Humbleton, if he will have me. I see now that Mr Pringle is delaying because he does not feel that way about me. So there is no reason why I shouldn't—'

'Don't be ridiculous, Harriet,' I ground out.

'But it will secure our home.' Her voice quivered. 'And after all, I was his first choice.'

'Neither of us should be marrying him,' I said through gritted teeth.

'Poverty isn't romantic, Fliss. It is frightening. I have no wish to see either of us ... lose our way.' She lowered her voice. 'I have been reading a novel that goes into some detail about what happens to girls like that.'

'Indeed, I assume it did not come from Mr Austen's library?'

'No, cousin Erica sent me her friend's copy of *Fanny Hill*, and I have spent the last few days perusing it. It is shocking. Worst of all, there is even a character called Harriet.' She let out a shrill mirthless laugh, which made George toss his head around.

I shushed him and tightened the reins. I hadn't read *Fanny Hill*, but I knew the gist of what it contained since it had been banned. What was Erica thinking sending her that!

'I doubt Aunt would let us become prostitutes, dearest,' I said gently. 'Even if we had to reside with her and live on bread and gruel, it would be better than marrying Mr Humbleton.'

I felt more hopeful on both our behalves. Perhaps we wouldn't thrive in the future or achieve our wish of marrying for love, but at least we wouldn't sink to selling our bodies on the street!

* * *

The next few days were horrible. Papa and I were hardly speaking, which made for tense mealtimes, and Mr Humbleton redoubled his efforts to woo me. I started receiving badly written poems pushed underneath our bedroom door three times a day. In fact, I started being able to tell the time by them.

'Look, another one,' I said to Harriet, brandishing his latest artistic effort posted on the dot of seven in the evening. The verses were usually short and to the point and consisted of him trying to rhyme 'Felicity' with different words and phrases. So far, there had been 'will you be', 'beautifully', 'uncommonly', 'you and me', and 'dreamily'. But I didn't find it clever. Instead, it was rather creepy.

Harriet read it and winced. 'Hardly lyrical,' she agreed.

After her willingness to sacrifice herself to Mr Humbleton on my behalf, I'd wholeheartedly forgiven her, and we'd formed an alliance against the men in the household. As she said, we were both in the same boat, unprotected and in peril, so we had to stick together. She'd taken to reading me particularly appalling passages in the well-thumbed copy of *Fanny Hill*, ones that highlighted Fanny's vulnerability and servitude. So we were in a constant state of mental aggression towards the male sex. It was a good thing that Mr Pringle or Mr Fitzroy did not write or visit during this time as they may have been subjected to our ill temper.

However, a letter for Harriet did duly arrive from Ashbury Manor, but it was not from Mr Pringle. It was from his cousin Rosalind Whiteley, inviting us for afternoon tea two days hence. It was obviously the work of Mr Fitzroy dutifully conveying Harriet's wish to become better acquainted with the lady.

'What do you think, Fliss? Is your ankle strong enough?'

I nodded. 'Yes, I can walk quite well now. But we should take the buggy to save our strength ...' *For the ordeal*, I added privately.

'I shall write to her forthwith,' said Harriet, dimples appearing in her cheeks. 'What fun!'

Fanny Hill was put away, and Harriet commenced reading a much milder romance while I grappled with an ever-growing pile of poetry. When my cousin had finally taken himself back to Hertfordshire, single and unattached, I would burn them in the back garden and consider myself blessed for escaping his clutches. Until then, I dreaded the sound of folded paper scraping under the door.

It was with a large helping of trepidation, but also a pinch of gratefulness for an escape, that Harriet and I set off to Ashbury Manor in our best day dresses and bonnets. Mr Humbleton offered to drive us over in his carriage, but I knew he'd invite himself to join us, and Rosalind would have no choice but to grudgingly accept. So we evaded him, not directly, but by telling him we were leaving at two o'clock and then leaving ten minutes before he was ready. I felt no guilt. A poem was sure to be posted under my door at seven o'clock with the word 'miserably' rhyming with my name, I had no doubt.

The day was fine and clear, and George was behaving himself for once by not pulling at the reins and moving faster than a snail's pace, so I was enjoying the outing.

As we clopped into the drive that led to Ashbury, Harriet said breathlessly, 'Do you think the gentlemen will be there?'

She'd voiced the question I'd been wondering myself. 'No clue,' I said nonchalantly. 'Even if they are, it is of no concern to us.'

But the rapid escalation of my heart as we came to a stop in front of the manor said otherwise.

Rosalind greeted us cordially when we were shown in by the footman, enquiring after our health and our journey. But as she swept us efficiently along to her private parlour for tea, I sensed there was an ulterior motive to her invitation. Of Mr Pringle and Mr Fitzroy, there was no sign; the house was strangely silent and bereft of their presence. Had she cleared them out on purpose? I didn't trust her one jot, and I braced myself for some kind of unpleasantness.

'You can tidy up over there.' Rosalind waved a hand to a small alcove that held a coat rack, a mirror, and a shelf with several bottles of scent. Harriet and I obediently shrugged off our pelisses, untied our bonnets, and checked our hair in the mirror. I sniffed the bottles and spritzed some jasmine scent behind my ears. Why not indeed?

Rosalind's parlour was a lovely room, well appointed for a lady to receive visitors. I particularly liked the flowered meadow wall mural, the twin turquoise-and-gold-striped settees, and the white gossamer curtains, which billowed in the afternoon breeze. I could quite happily spend a lot of time in a room like this. I guessed Harriet could too as I heard her sigh enviously as she looked around.

'Which tea would you like?' asked Rosalind. 'I have congou or lapsang souchong that I brought with me from London or chamomile and mint if you prefer herbal.'

The first two sounded exotic and, as we drank common black tea at home, unfamiliar. 'Um, mint would be lovely, thank you,' I said, deciding to play it safe. Harriet murmured that she would have chamomile.

Rosalind pulled on a bell cord and ordered a teapot of boiling water and a 'selection of petits fours' when the servant appeared. 'I have my own cups and saucers here,' she explained, gesturing to a sideboard where a delicate bone china tea set was laid out.

To my mind, she seemed very settled at Ashbury, having brought a tea set with her. But perhaps that's what upper-class ladies did when they travelled because they could not trust the quality of teacups in the country?

After the business of pouring the tea and choosing from a

plate of petits fours was done, Harriet and I perched on one settee, and Rosalind on the other. I bit into my small iced cake with a sugar rose. It had an apricot filling and was delicious, but tiny. I eyed the rest of the plate and wondered if it would be rude to ask for another, but I didn't want to appear greedy as Rosalind was having only one. Instead, I concentrated on sipping my tea, which was very good— smooth, piquant, and delightfully ... minty.

'Well, isn't this lovely? Thank you both for coming. I was starting to feel quite bored here with no other females to talk to. So when Max told me you wished for a proper introduction, I was delighted.'

She smoothed her turquoise silk dress, which I noticed happened to perfectly match the settee. *Perhaps she'd got a batch deal,* I thought a touch snidely.

'It is our pleasure,' said Harriet politely. 'I am sorry that we didn't get a chance to meet at the ball. Your cousin kept me too occupied with dancing. I had very sore feet at the end of the evening.'

Rosalind's eyes narrowed slightly. 'Indeed,' she said dryly. 'I shall scold him for that.'

'Oh no ...' Harriet began, but Rosalind's lips curled in the semblance of a smile, and it was apparent she was only joking. My sister sipped her chamomile tea and stayed quiet. *Good girl, Harriet,* I thought. *Keep your feelings for him in check.*

The lady turned her attention to me. 'I do believe congratulations are in order, Felicity,' she said, smiling and tilting her head.

I stared at her blankly. 'Pardon?'

'Your recent engagement? To Mr Humbleton? Max mentioned it after his visit the other day. Poor dear, he seemed rather in a state. Apparently, he'd dropped cream sponge on his trousers. Most unfortunate.'

My mouth dropped open slightly. *What?*

Rosalind glanced at my left hand and tsked. 'But no ring? Shame on your fiancé for neglecting that!'

I managed to collect my wits before she could continue further in this vein. 'But I am not engaged, madam. Mr Fitzroy is very much mistaken about what he heard.'

Rosalind looked astonished. 'Not engaged? But Max told me you were, and he has perfect hearing.' She looked enquiringly at me, and I fumed.

Oh, this was too bad of him! Why had he said anything to her at all? Had he been in a fit of ill temper when he'd returned?

I tried to speak calmly. 'What he heard was Mr Humbleton saying he was my *intended* husband, which does not mean the matter has been settled—far from it.'

Rosalind tilted her head the other way. 'So it is just a matter of negotiation?'

'Not at all,' I said, gritting my teeth.

'Perhaps we should change the subject,' murmured Harriet, sensing by my tone that I was becoming upset.

'Of course,' said Rosalind, widening her eyes and looking at each of us in mock alarm. 'Please do have another petit four. They will be discarded if they're not eaten. Cook makes them fresh each day.'

She proffered the plate, and silently, I took two of the tiny cakes. Popping both of them into my mouth, I chewed angrily, the sugar doing nothing to sweeten me up to Lady Whiteley. Is that why she'd invited us here, to grill me on my supposed engagement? Or to find out how Harriet felt about Mr Pringle? It seemed she'd achieved both goals before we'd even finished our first cup of tea.

'Well,' she said, seemingly recovered from her faux pas, 'it appears I shall have to scold Max too for spreading false information.' She gave a tinkling laugh.

'Do not trouble yourself on my behalf.' I swallowed quickly, imagining his irritation at being reminded of that Blackburn girl flinging cake at him. 'It was just a misunderstanding.'

'Are you worried he might get angry? He may look fierce, but I can handle him. Besides, he tends to make special allowances for me.'

She smiled secretively and looked down at her slim white

fingers. Her right hand was adorned with a delicate silver signet ring. Her left hand was bare.

I understood instantly what this was. Rosalind was conveying in no uncertain terms that *she* was the lady Mr Fitzroy was interested in, not I.

My spirits deflated because, of course, I could not compete with her. I was a drab bird. The expensively decorated room began to feel like a gilded cage, and I decided I needed some air. 'Madam, forgive me, I ... I need to use your privy.'

'Of course, mint tea has that effect on me too. That's why I chose the congou. Go through the small door on the left, and that will take you outside to the shack. I apologise in advance—the plumbing facilities here are medieval.' She shuddered. 'That is part of the reason I am going back to London shortly.'

'When do you leave?' enquired Harriet, sounding none too bereft about her new friend going.

'In a few days,' she said. 'I believe Max intends to accompany me.' I couldn't miss the supercilious glance she shot my way as I got up to leave the room.

I stood in the hallway outside, taking some deep calming breaths. The woman was pure poison! But my sense of humour returned, and I had to laugh at her not-so-subtle attempts to warn me off Mr Fitzroy.

He made 'special allowances' for her? He had called on *me* and made no mention of being intimately acquainted with her, so it was more likely he was politely putting up with her for his friend's sake.

But if it was true that he was leaving for London shortly, then that was that. There was no point thinking or dreaming about him anymore. Strangely, though, I fancied I could smell his deliciously spicy male scent wafting past my nose. Bah, it was probably just furniture polish!

Chapter 15

I had to agree with Rosalind: the privy *was* medieval. As I squatted in the foul-smelling shack, I tried but failed to picture her using it. And what about Mr Fitzroy? Had his bottom touched this seat? I really had to stop thinking about him, especially where his buttocks were concerned.

I'd just come out of the privy and started back towards the house when the man himself strode around the side of the house from the direction of the stables. He pulled up short upon seeing me with a startled look on his face.

'Mr Fitzroy,' I said, feeling equally shocked. Composing himself, he bowed, and I returned it somewhat stiffly.

'Miss Blackburn, good day. I have been out riding with Evan,' he said as if he needed an explanation for being there. He glanced behind me at the privy. 'Surely, you didn't ...?'

'I did. It was not a pleasant experience.'

'But we have a privy upstairs, complete with flushing water. Why did Rosalind direct you out here?'

So the lack of facilities she was bleating on about was a blatant lie! 'No doubt because it is closer to her parlour and

I was in a hurry after drinking a large cup of mint tea,' I said tightly.

He nodded and thankfully dropped the subject of the privy but then took up another that was even worse. 'Miss Blackburn, I left in haste the other day and forgot my manners,' he said, shifting awkwardly. 'Congratulations. I wish you and Mr Humbleton every happiness.'

The firm set of his mouth and coldness in his eyes suggested otherwise, and I longed for it to be because he was perturbed about my being off the market rather than just opposed to marriage in general.

A tightness rose within my chest, and I knew I had to say something. There might never be another chance, even if he had set his sights on another.

O no, it is an ever-fixèd mark
That looks on tempests and is never shaken.

I drew myself up to my full height and looked him squarely in the eye. 'Sir, no matter what you heard that man say, I am not engaged to him. And I do not wish to be, not now or ever.'

He stared at me.

'But you are. I even heard it in the village.'

I let out a huff of impatience.

'And you listen to gossip, I suppose? I am telling you now, plainly and directly, I do not wish to be tied to him!'

Mr Fitzroy let out a breath, and the atmosphere around him seemed suddenly less ferocious. 'So what am I to think of it then?'

'Do not think of it because it doesn't exist! Even if Papa ...' I broke off, not wanting to discuss my private affairs further. 'Excuse me, I must go in. The others will be wondering where I am.'

I made a movement towards the door, but Mr Fitzroy stepped towards me.

'So you are really not engaged to him?'

'No. I would rather sell my body on the street,' I replied without thinking and blushed hotly when Mr Fitzroy's expression darkened (damn Harriet for reading *Fanny Hill* to me).

He raked his gaze over my face. 'Let us hope it will not come to that,' he murmured.

Within the house, I heard Harriet calling my name.

'Please excuse me, I must go. My sister needs me.'

Mr Fitzroy inclined his head. 'Good day, Miss Blackburn. Our conversation has been most enlightening.'

Had it? I now felt more confused than ever.

He strode away, leaving my emotions in a whirl. With a shaking hand, I opened the small door and stepped into the hallway immediately encountering Harriet.

'Fliss! There you are. We should go. Rosalind is coming down with a headache and wishes to rest.'

'With pleasure,' I replied, relieved. 'Do you think she'll notice if we steal the rest of the petits fours?'

Harriet was in a jubilant mood on the journey home because Mr Pringle had made an appearance before we'd left. He had begged us to stay longer, and when Rosalind said we could not, he delayed Harriet in conversation for a good ten minutes (much to Rosalind's annoyance) and then helped her into the buggy. Apparently, according to Harriet, his hand had lingered in hers as if he hadn't wanted to let it go.

'He is so lovely.' I heard her give a little dreamy sigh as we clopped steadily down the road. 'And what good timing! A moment later, and we would have missed him. His pernicious cousin was not at all happy that he was talking to me.'

I glanced at her, surprised. She never usually spoke badly of anyone—at least I'd never heard her. 'Well done, Harriet. I think that's the first time you've actually called someone out on their faults. It's quite refreshing to hear.'

She coloured. 'I shouldn't have said that, but she's just so awful. I cannot believe she's Evan's cousin since he is so amiable.'

I laughed out loud, and she huffed a chuckle.

'It's just a pity Mr Fitzroy wasn't there,' she continued. 'I'm sure he would have liked to have seen you.'

I shrugged dismissively and clicked to George. He was jerking his head, as if hearing Mr Fitzroy's name disturbed him as much as it did me.

'I am glad he wasn't,' I stated, declining to mention my encounter with him by the privy. 'It would have been awkward. Anyway, I hope Mr Pringle does not delay any further with his proposal.'

Harriet jigged up and down excitedly. 'I hope so too!'

'Yes. Otherwise, you'll be old and grey by the time he gets around to it!' I quipped, and she whacked my arm good-naturedly.

Unfortunately, Harriet's high spirits and even higher hopes were soundly dashed when she received a letter from Mr Pringle at breakfast the next morning. It was just us as Papa and Mr Humbleton had eaten earlier and gone out on some errand.

I knew the letter was bad news because Harriet immediately seemed to deflate upon reading it.

'What is it?' I asked.

Silently, she handed it over, her eyes sad and her mouth pinched.

Oh no, I thought. *What now?*

Rapidly, I perused the contents, and my heart sank. Mr Pringle was escorting his cousin back to London forthwith and would be staying there for a few weeks to partake of what was left of the season. But he said he hoped to find time to write to Harriet from there, depending on his schedule.

'Do not give up, love. At least he plans to write,' I said reassuringly. But it must have been a cruel blow as, thanks to me, she had been expecting a proposal.

'I ... I think I will go to my room. I have a bad headache all of a sudden,' she murmured.

'Finish your breakfast at least.' Her roll was half eaten, and there was a cup of tea cooling. But she shook head and left the room looking so depressed that my heart bled for her. I wanted to wring Mr Pringle's neck.

I strongly suspected pernicious Lady Whiteley had had a hand in this latest manoeuvre. Either she hadn't been able to coerce Mr Fitzroy to go with her to London, or she'd perceived that her cousin was about to propose. Whatever the reason, it made me extremely angry that she was trying to keep him away from Harriet and that Mr Pringle had let himself be so easily manipulated. It didn't bode well for Harriet's future, unless he could locate his backbone.

I spent the rest of the day comforting Harriet as her emotional state was shaky at best, and there were a few tears to be dried. I tried to bolster her morale as much as I could, but I was not a fortune teller. Whether Mr Pringle would propose, I could not foresee; all I could do was utter words of reassurance and offer comforting hugs to ease the pain of separation.

Not surprisingly, by late afternoon, I also had a splitting headache. We both pleaded ill for supper, so Mary served us in our room: vegetable broth, boiled eggs, soft cheese, and freshly baked bread, along with a jam tart each for afters.

'A little nourishment does wonders for the soul, Harriet,' I said, my mouth watering as I surveyed the spread laid out on her nightstand. 'You'll feel much more cheerful after eating a good meal.'

'I suppose I could manage a mouthful or two of broth,' Harriet said forlornly.

However, once beginning, she discovered there was nothing wrong with her appetite; and we both ate heartily until there were crumbs.

Though it was barely dark, we retired early, Harriet again reading out bits of *Fanny Hill* (she had picked it up again in defiance) until we both grew weary and she snuffed out the candle. I fell into a deep dreamless slumber, only to wake with a start some hours later, with a full moon shining brightly through the window as we had forgotten to draw the curtains.

Careful not to disturb Harriet, I stood by the window, looking out at the silvery illuminated fields. A snatch of an off-key tune floated to my ears from outside the window, and I realised it was this that had roused me, not the moonlight. Someone was doing an excellent job of murdering a ditty. I listened for a bit. Then the singing abruptly ceased, and I heard my name being called, albeit drunkenly.

'Felishity, O wherefore art thou Felishity ...'

Oh good Lord, it was Samuel, and he was soused! Had something gone wrong with Miss Matlock, and he had decided to turn to me for solace? I had to silence him before he woke everyone up and made a complete fool of himself.

Throwing on a warm housecoat over my chemise, I quickly thrust bare feet into boots, tiptoed downstairs, and let myself silently out the side door.

'Samuel? Where are you?' I called in a low voice when I reached the field as there was no one in sight. An owl hooted far off in the distance; then there was a rustling from a nearby thicket of trees. A tall figure emerged and stood there, swaying.

'Whosh Samuel?' it slurred.

With the effect of moonlight shining upon his dark hair

and angular features, it was easy to recognise who it was. But it was also quite shocking.

'Mr Fitzroy, what on earth are you doing here?' I hissed as he walked or, should I say, staggered towards me. He was clutching a wine bottle, and as I watched, he tipped it to his lips and took a generous swig.

'Ah, Felishity, exshallent! Jush the woman I wanted to shee.'

'You did?' I said nervously, for there was an element of the ruffian about him. He wore a dark overcoat, but his cravat was missing, and his white shirt was open at the neck.

'Felishity delishity,' he growled huskily.

I shivered, drawing my coat around me tightly.

'I do not know what you are doing, Mr Fitzroy, but you need to go home,' I whispered to him.

He glared at me. 'I will do noshing of the sort!' he said loudly.

'Shhhh!'

He put a finger to his lips and repeated it in a mock whisper, which made me want to giggle. His antics, despite being strange and wild, were starting to amuse me. I had never seen him like this.

'Does Mr Pringle know you've been into his wine cellar?'

'Pffft. It ish only a shmidgen. He will not notish.'

He tipped the bottle to his mouth again and took a swallow, whereupon some wine spilled out and dribbled down his shirt front. He didn't seem to care. I raised my eyebrows. Judging from the way he was weaving around and now the magenta spillage, he had drunk rather more than a smidgen.

He'd obviously been left to his own devices alone at the manor, thanks to the departure of Rosalind and Evan. But what had happened for him to hit the bottle like there was no tomorrow?

'Come closher, Felishity. I want to tell you a shecret.' He beckoned me over with an exaggerated motion. Understandably, I was somewhat reluctant to go near him. Mr Fitzroy in this state was wholly unpredictable.

I approached cautiously, like he was a wild animal liable to spring at me without warning. The closer I edged, the stronger the stench of wine fumes became.

'Mish Blackburn.' He bowed unsteadily.

'Mr Fitzroy.' I returned the bow, playing along.

He gazed at me intently as if memorising my face.

'Each time I encounter you, I am either wet or covered in cream,' he muttered. 'I hardly know what shtate I'll find myshelf in next.'

I stifled a laugh. 'Very true. But you hardly needed to come all this way to tell me that.'

An unreadable expression crossed his features. Then without warning, he sank to one knee. I blinked.

'What are you doing?'

But he ignored me and clasped the wine bottle to his chest with one hand and flung out the other like he was in an opera.

'Mish Felishity Blackburn, would you do me the greatisht honour of becoming my knife.' He gave a strangled cough. 'I mean *wife.*'

I stared down at him. 'You don't mean that.'

'I do, I truly do,' he implored and emitted a tiny burp to emphasise it.

'Mr Fitzroy, you are being ridiculous. Please leave. Immediately.' I didn't know whether to laugh or feel insulted.

'No, not until you give me a shtraight answer.' His wine-stained lips pressed together in a firm line, and I had a feeling he wasn't going to go quietly.

His eyes, although glazed, were beseeching as he looked up at me.

I wavered. Was he being serious? Or playing the fool? Of course the idea of being married to him was something I had considered, even coveted. But to be proposed to like this? Was it even legally binding if I said yes?

I did not know what to do.

Perhaps I should just ... run away.

Seeing me take a hesitant step backwards, he grabbed me tightly round the waist and buried his face in my midriff.

'Mr Fitzroy, let go of me!' I hissed. But he held me tightly, and I couldn't move.

'Pretty please, marry me?' came the muffled enquiry from the depths of my chemise.

I wiggled, but he wouldn't budge. I could feel the muscles in his arms flexing as he attempted to restrain me. I did not feel afraid, in fact the opposite. But as he would not remember this in the cold light of day, there was only one thing for it to make him release me.

'All right,' I said.

There was a silence; then a deep shuddering sigh escaped him. He removed his face from my chemise and looked up at me; on it was a wide joyful smile. I didn't think I'd ever seen him smile like that before; it was something to behold, even if he was pickled as a newt. I couldn't help smiling back.

'Truly?' he asked, his voice full of wonder.

'Truly,' I replied, patting his head placatingly like he was a little boy. 'Now shall we go to the house, and I will make you a cup of coffee?' *For I think you need a strong one*, I added silently.

'Yesh, a mosht exshellent idea.'

With my help, he hoisted himself up, and I led the way towards the house. I kept checking behind to see if he was following, and he was doing so. But at one point, he must have been confused and turned left instead of right.

I clicked my fingers at him. 'This way, Mr Fitzroy,' I whispered. 'You're going to our horse's stable.'

He stopped with a jolt. 'Ah, lead on, fair maiden!' he called, and I shushed him hurriedly. Was bringing him into the house wise? What if he woke up Papa and Mr Humbleton? But there was no other alternative. I could not leave him in the field; he might come to harm. And I did not particularly fancy accompanying him to Ashbury Manor at this time of night.

We went through the side door and into the kitchen, and I lit a couple of candles while Mr Fitzroy slouched against the doorframe, looking worse for wear.

'You can sit there at the table while I make the coffee,' I whispered, pointing to a chair.

He nodded and launched off in the general direction, but in doing so, he knocked into the edge of the sideboard. 'Oh, pleash do forgive me,' he slurred and bowed to it politely, which nearly set me off into a fit of giggles.

Jane would love hearing about this, but I knew I could never tell her; it would end up in her story, and Mr Fitzroy would be extremely ashamed of himself when he sobered up. I would hate for his behaviour to be made common knowledge to the village if Jane's scribbles fell into the wrong hands.

Mr Fitzroy plonked himself into a chair and laid his head on the table sideways with his arms hanging limply underneath.

Poor dear, he was in a bad way. I bustled around, stoking the stove fire, which luckily still had a couple of glowing embers, and putting the kettle on the stove to boil.

No one drank coffee in our house but Papa, so I wasn't exactly sure how to prepare it. Retrieving the tin of ground beans from the pantry, I added a generous measure to a cup. When it was ready, I poured in boiling water and stirred the evil-looking black brew. Yet it emitted a rich pleasant aroma, and I knew it was what he needed, especially as his eyes had already drooped shut.

I nudged his shoulder. 'Mr Fitzroy, sit up and drink this.'

His eyes shot open at once, and he lifted his head off the table.

'Here, it will restore you to your senses.' I held the steaming cup to his lips, and he dutifully took a small sip.

'Hot,' he murmured.

'Take another, but slowly,' I urged.

He obeyed and gingerly swallowed. 'Good,' he stated with a nod.

It appeared all he could manage now were one-syllable words!

I made him keep drinking the coffee until the cup was drained, and he leaned back in the chair with his eyes closed. His face was flushed bright red—whether from the heat of the coffee or the wine, I wasn't sure. Either way, I suddenly regretted my decision to give him strong coffee. Perhaps I should have given him ginger tea instead?

Concerned, I felt his forehead, which was bathed in sweat and overly warm to the touch.

'Mmm, that feelsh nice,' he muttered as my cool hand pressed on his hot skin.

I moved the back of my hand to the side of his face, feeling the rasp of his stubble, and he sighed. 'Very, very nice.'

At this close range, I could smell the mixture of coffee and wine on his breath. His full lips were moist and parted.

Feeling my gaze upon him, Mr Fitzroy's bleary eyes opened and locked on mine. 'Kish me,' he murmured.

Chapter 16

Kissing Mr Fitzroy was not a good idea. He was in a vulnerable state. Also, he had just asked me to marry him, which was proof he was not in his right mind. But despite this, he was still the most attractive man I had ever laid eyes on; and I could not deny that, by now, I was harbouring tender feelings for him. So I decided to oblige him a little.

I lowered my lips to his and gave him a chaste kiss. To my mind, it could hardly even be described as a kiss as it was so brief. He must have thought so too as he instantly said, 'More.'

'Well, if you insist,' I replied with a smile, knowing he was going to be angry about this in the morning, but I could not help myself.

I lowered my lips again; and we shared a longer, deeper kiss, which caused my heart to flutter madly. Kissing him in the flesh was even better than in my fantasy—though in my fantasy, he hadn't been rollicking drunk. But this worked in my favour as he was less inhibited than he might have been sober and was most eager to insert his tongue in my mouth.

One of his hands came up to entwine in my hair, and I

gently caressed the soft down at the back of his neck. After a while, I pulled away as the position of leaning down to him was making my back ache. 'Mmm, your lipsh tashte schweeter than wine,' he slurred.

'Of which you have had a lot of,' I quipped.

He chuckled, which gave way to a hiccup.

I made to fetch him some water, but he captured me round the waist and insisted I kiss him again. I was rather liking this impetuous Mr Fitzroy, who was giving into his spontaneous passion rather than curtailing it. Caught up in his fervour of recklessness, I happily did so, plying his lips with my own and enjoying the pleasurable plundering of our tongues. Therefore, I was hardly taking notice of where his large hands were until one landed on my right buttock.

'Mr Fitzroy!' I gasped.

He simply gazed back at me with an innocent look.

I eyed him suspiciously. Was he still drunk after all that coffee? Or did he suddenly look brighter and more lucid?

He grinned at me. 'Please, call me Max. My given name is Maximilian. But it's a bit of a mouthful, so everyone calls me Max. And I think by now we are friends, are we not?'

Hmm, he now sounded completely sober to my ears! His hand stayed firmly on my bottom, massaging it a little. and I raised my eyebrows. *Perhaps a little more than friends, Max ...*

I nodded. 'Very well. I suppose so, especially after the lake and the cake.' *And the kissing and your hand on my derriere ...*

He chuckled. 'I like that—the lake and the cake.' His free hand grasped my other buttock, and I bit my lip.

'Max,' I chided softly, liking saying his name.

'I promise I will not compromise you,' he said, his tone thickening. I did not believe him in the slightest but allowed him to kiss me again while he kneaded my buttocks with his warm hands, and I grew rather light-headed with desire.

Where all this would have ended, I do not know. But he abruptly pulled his lips away from mine, looking pale.

'I feel slightly ... odd. I am afraid I might be ...'

He made a retching noise and vomited violently onto the flagstone floor, some of it splashing up and catching the bottom of my chemise.

I sprang out of the way and waited until he'd finished heaving, my hand lightly rubbing his back.

When it was over, Max wiped his mouth with his hand. 'Oh my god, I am disgusting.' He sounded distressed.

'No,' I said quickly. 'It is my fault. I should not have given you coffee. There was too much acidity in it.'

'Even so ...' He gazed at the scarlet mess on the floor in horror. Luckily, he'd managed to miss his trousers, or that would have been another pair stained.

'Stay there. I will fetch a cloth.'

I hurried to wet a clean rag and used it to wipe his face and hands.

'Perhaps you should go to the parlour and rest,' I said.

'But ...' He gestured to the puddle of vomit, and I shook my head. 'I will clean it up.' How to do that, I was not entirely sure. But I knew Mary had a mop and bucket. I had seen her use them.

'I am so sorry.'

'I hope my kissing didn't cause it,' I joked.

'Not at all.' He looked at me earnestly, like he wanted to resume our intimacy, but there was no way I was kissing him now. Besides, dawn was merely hours away, and I needed to mop the kitchen floor before Sue came down to start breakfast!

Depositing Max into the parlour, I helped him remove his boots; and he lay on the sofa, looking tired but snug with Harriet's embroidered cushion under his head and a blanket tucked around him. 'Do you think you will be ill again?' I asked, checking the room for a suitable vessel, but he shook his head.

'All right.'

I made to go, but he grabbed my hand. 'Thank you, Felicity.'

'You are welcome ... Max.'

Saying his name aloud sounded strange, but nice.

He squeezed my hand and yawned.

'Sleep,' I said, squeezing his hand back, then gently withdrawing my fingers from his. 'You will feel better in the morning.' *Well, apart from a sore head ...*

He nodded, closed his eyes, and instantly fell asleep. He must have been exhausted.

By the time I had finished cleaning the floor (after gagging several times), birds were tweeting the dawn chorus, and I was on my last legs too.

I crept upstairs to our room, where I stripped off my soiled chemise and carefully pulled out the dresser drawer to get a fresh one. But it squeaked, sounding very loud in the stillness.

Harriet stirred in bed. 'Is everything all right, Fliss?' came her sleepy mumble from behind me.

'Yes, dearest. Go back to sleep.'

She turned over, and I let out a breath. *If she only knew what a night I'd had!*

Slipping into the ice-cold sheets on my side of the bed, I shivered for a bit but soon warmed up. As I drifted off, I thought about Max. It was comforting to know he was safely ensconced downstairs in the parlour and not lying sozzled in a field where he may have been trampled by a wandering cow!

* * *

When I awoke, the sun was climbing a cloudless blue sky, and Harriet was not there. I lay there for a second to orient my fuzzy brain. Then one piercing thought entered: *Max! Was he still here?*

I flung back the covers and dressed quickly, not bothering to wash or pin up my hair. He had seen me like this already and had thought well of it, if him kissing me enthusiastically and kneading my bottom were anything to go by. My face flushed pink at the memory as I ran downstairs, eager to see him.

But the parlour was as empty as a church on a Monday. The grey blanket was folded neatly on the arm of the sofa and the embroidered pillow placed alongside it. I groaned. Surely, he wasn't having breakfast with Papa, Harriet, and Mr Humbleton?

I took up the blanket, intending to return it to its original position by the fireplace. But as I did so, a square of paper fell out of its folds. It had 'FB' scrawled on the front, so I assumed it was for me.

My hand tingled as I held it. Max had written me a letter. But why was it penned in red crayon?

4 September 1796

Dear Miss Blackburn,

I left at first light when the birds started chirping, loudly might I add, which did not help my headache. But I have only myself to blame.

Madam, I am wholly and utterly ashamed of myself. I apologise profusely for my uncouth behaviour and lack of propriety. I promise you that it shall never happen again.

You may recall, as I do now with much embarrassment, that I made a proposal of marriage to you. That you accepted it is wondrous under the nefarious circumstances, and I am in awe that you did not deny me and run for the hills. I can only surmise that you were attempting to pacify me.

I shall return to London forthwith to consult with my lawyer. Do not despair. I will resolve the matter hastily and write to you anon when it has been done.

Again, my sincere apologies for any damage caused (to your house, clothing, and your senses). I will send funds to cover the first two and pray that the latter are soon fully restored. Thank you for your kindness in caring for me when I was in a deplorable state.

I would write more, but this crayon is now a mere stub. (Please do thank your sister for the use of her utensil and drawing paper, which I found in the desk.)

Yrs,
Max Fitzroy

Indeed, there was a red smudge after his signature flourish, as if the rest of the crayon had crumbled. I was half impressed despite myself that he had found the mental agility to write such a letter as well as remembering to date and sign it. If I had been him, I doubt I could have managed it; a mere 'Apologies, madam, and thank you for the blanket' would have been the lot.

As such, I had no idea what to make of this confusing epistle: 'I will resolve the matter hastily.' What did that mean? I read the letter again, and as its meaning became clearer, my mood soured.

The formal tone as well as calling me 'Miss Blackburn' rather than 'Felicity' like he had last night suggested he was brushing our newfound intimacy under the carpet for the sake of propriety. And it went without saying that he was relying on my discretion about the drinking and its mucky aftermath.

Oh, Mr Fitzroy had proven himself to be cad, a rake of the worst kind—one that played the part of a gentleman! Not only had he stolen kisses from me. He had also stolen my heart, cooked it, and handed it back to me steaming on a platter. But what could I do? Write to him and demand that he honour his proposal? It would solve the current dilemma with my cousin, but something would not let me do such a thing. It would be trapping him in the worst way, and I did not want to be married to him like that—I wanted him to give his affection freely. But his letter told me that that was the last thing I should expect.

I started to tear up the paper, but something in me couldn't bring myself to complete the action. Folding it tightly, I tucked it into the top of my dress for safe keeping in case I wanted to peruse it again later.

With a sigh, I made my way to the dining room to find out if breakfast was still laid out. If not, I would have to go to the kitchen and beg a roll and butter from Sue— something I'd rather not do after the intimacy that had occurred in there between Max and me; it would be an all-too-painful reminder. To my surprise, Harriet, Papa, and Mr Humbleton were still in the dining room. But the breakfast had been cleared, and there was nothing but a lone teapot and teacups on the sideboard.

'Ah, Felicity, finally,' said Papa when he saw me. 'Come in and sit down. We've been waiting for you.'

I glanced at Harriet, and she managed a thin smile. Meanwhile, Mr Humbleton inclined his head, saying nothing. Something was up. I could fairly sense it. Ignoring my rumbling stomach, I sat down timorously in the nearest chair.

'What is it, Papa?' I asked.

As a reply, he reached into the breast pocket of his jacket and brought out a thick cream-coloured piece of paper that had been folded neatly into thirds. He unfolded it and pushed it over to me, and I saw it was covered with an official-looking cursive.

'Please read it and sign your name at the bottom,' said Papa, sounding weary. A quill and ink were produced and made ready for my use.

Heart hammering in my chest, I picked up the document and stared at it. The first sentence leapt out and pierced me like an arrow: 'I, Felicity Anne Blackburn, agree to be married to Percival Arthur Humbleton under the following terms ...'

Immediately, I dropped it like a hot potato. 'I am not signing *this*,' I said, glaring at Mr Humbleton, who smiled impassively.

'If you would be kind enough to read the *entire*

document, cousin,' he said. His tone was smooth, but strong and left no room for argument.

Papa nodded at me. 'Please, Felicity.' I picked up the paper again and scanned the terms of the marriage, which were not too lengthy but clearly stated that Mr Humbleton and I would be man and wife in name only and, most surprising of all, *there would be no conjugal relations, and we would have separate rooms.*

My eyes widened. What in God's good name?

Astounded, I stared at Mr Humbleton. 'What is this?'

'Your father has worked the terms of our union in your favour, and I've been generous enough to agree to it,' he said as if that explained it. All it did was make my head swim with confusion.

'In my favour?' I said slowly, looking now to Papa.

'Yes, my dear,' he said gently. 'This arrangement protects you and looks out for your best interests—you will not only have financial security but also personal freedom. See this line here.'

He reached over and pointed out the line in question, which affirmed that my cousin would have no authority over my actions as long those actions were in accordance with a good moral standing. I surmised that to mean I was not to participate in any type of extramarital affair as long as my cousin was alive and kicking.

'So I would be gaining money, security, and personal

freedom, but not love?' I clarified.

'Love is a commodity some can enjoy, but most cannot afford,' said Mr Humbleton sagely.

I narrowed my eyes at him. 'So much for trying to win my heart with poetry,' I said flatly and saw that, at least, he had the good grace to squirm. But it still did not make sense. 'Cousin, I can see how this arrangement would benefit me since I am not particularly inclined to have children. But why would you agree to it when you have so much to lose?'

My question was met with blank-faced silence. Papa cleared his throat. 'If I may attempt to explain to her,' he said. Mr Humbleton nodded abruptly once and looked out of the window, a faint blush rising in his cheeks.

I waited for Papa to speak, but he took his time, as if wanting to choose his words carefully. He began haltingly, 'There are some people who do not fit within the narrow confines of society's conventions ... Those people—through no fault of their own, might I add—find themselves drawn to other people who society deems unworthy. But, and I do believe this, we are still all God's children.' Father finished his convoluted speech and looked at me expectantly.

I frowned. What on earth was he trying to convey?

'Do you see what I mean, Felicity?' he asked somewhat impatiently, and I felt him urging me to understand so he would not have to speak in plainer terms.

My mind grappled with his intent. It was something to do with Mr Humbleton's embarrassment, him being different in some way, and why he deemed it important to marry me ... I thought hard about it, turning the pieces of the puzzle round and round in my brain, trying to fit them together. Then suddenly, they fell into place with a resounding click, and I gasped out loud. 'Oh!'

It was clear to me now why Mr Humbleton was not concerned about having me share his bed and why he sought a marriage that would be for appearances only. It was to satisfy his parish (or more perhaps to silence wagging tongues) that he wasn't a man with unholy desires. By marrying within the family, Mr Humbleton was in effect keeping his, and our, reputations intact as he knew I would not be able to tell anyone. Because if it got out, the scandal would ruin us all.

Yet another thing to keep secret from Jane ...

'I think I need a cup of tea,' I said faintly, looking around for the teapot.

'Let me,' said Harriet and poured me a full cup.

I sipped it gratefully, feeling rather stunned. My eyes flicked to my cousin, who couldn't seem to meet my gaze. I felt a slight softening towards him. He was, after all, in a dire predicament. One foot wrong, and he would hang. But he must move in those circles already.

'What about you?' I questioned. 'Surely, you are not planning on keeping me company in celibacy?'

Mr Humbleton coloured. 'It is true. I have ... *needs*. But I am used to being discreet,' he murmured.

I could not believe this.

I set my cup on the table. 'So you would be free to engage in extramarital dalliances, but I could not? That reeks of patriarchy!' I exclaimed. 'What if I am in love ... I mean, *fall* in love,' I corrected quickly, 'with someone? Am I to be denied that happiness?'

I was, of course, thinking about Max's proposal and his letter that itched against my bosom. If there was any time I had needed that epistle to be clear about where we stood, it was now. But he was obviously under the weather when he had penned it, and although a good letter, it was ambiguous as to what he intended.

'Papa?' I cried, starting to feel desperate.

He shook his head, tears forming in his eyes at my obvious distress, but he had no answer. Despite me initially thinking him cold-hearted in agreeing to this, I could now see that his heart was breaking, but that he was doing all he could to provide for me. Even if this marriage was abhorrent to him as well as me, I understood his reasoning for arranging it.

Panicking, I tried the Aunt Snelling angle.

'Papa, I do not need to be married,' I said urgently. 'If anything should happen to you, Harriet and I would live with Aunt. She would look after us. We do not need this house!'

Father swallowed. 'It's impossible. She cannot support three people on her small income. And as it's uncertain whether you'll ever receive another offer of marriage, there is no other way. You must marry Mr Humbleton to guarantee your security. I am sorry. Your poor mother—God rest her soul—begged me to look after you, and this is the best I can do to keep you from the streets.' His eyes filled with tears, which overflowed and ran down his cheeks; and it was this, I am sorry to say, that broke me.

Feeling like I was not in my own body, I picked up the quill, dipped it in the ink ... and signed my name in the space provided.

'Oh, Fliss!' Harriet, no doubt having been asked by the other two to be a witness to the signing, burst into tears and ran from the room.

I felt nothing but numb.

So this was my fate—to marry a man who had no affinity with the fairer sex, a man who liked men. I could not believe this was happening to me.

PART FOUR

A Story Is Born

Chapter 17

Mr Humbleton left for Hertfordshire immediately after breakfast. He said he wanted to start the wedding preparations and announce the news of his engagement to the parish. He appeared elated at his good fortune in securing a bride, even one that did not want him. In the contract he had stipulated a short two-month engagement. But after a verbal wrestling match involving emotional blackmail, I managed to persuade him, grudgingly, to alter it to three months. Our future living arrangement did not bode well. Unfortunately for me, Mr Humbleton was a man who liked to be in control, albeit passively. So I knew I would have to remind him constantly of the terms of the contract he'd agreed to—that he had *no control* over me as long as I was behaving properly. It made me tired just thinking about it.

Mary changed the linens on my bed, gave the room a good airing, and, at my bidding, strung up bunches of lavender. I began moving my books, dresses, and other belongings back in; and she helped me.

'What about these, miss?' she asked, holding out the small pile of Mr Humbleton's poems I had bound with string. 'Do you want them for your hope chest?'

'No. Please burn them,' I replied tightly. At this point in time, the word 'hope' was somewhat ironic.

Mary looked shocked that I would deign to burn poetry. But she dutifully took them outside, and a short time later, I smelt smoke wafting up through the open window from the back garden. It gave me a modicum of satisfaction to know those horrid poems had been incinerated.

The next day, the weather turned nasty; and a black cloud hung over Steventon, literally and figuratively. Denied my daily walk, thanks to the relentless rain, there was nothing to do but lie on the parlour sofa and stare listlessly at the crackling fire—and think of Mr Fitzroy. (I had reverted to calling him that in my mind rather than Max, which now felt too intimate since he had rejected me.)

Every now and again, I touched his letter, which I had taken to tucking into the top of my dress. It was a silly fancy, and I knew I should not cherish it so dearly, especially as it was no indication of his tender feelings towards me—instead quite the opposite. But as I lay there, thinking of him and wondering if he was in London and, if so, what he was doing, the pain of his leaving and my newly engaged state to Mr Humbleton grew so bad that I let out a small groan. I knew I should be bold and cast his letter into the fire to cut the tie that was binding me to him. (Also, as I had read it umpteen times, the crayon was starting to smudge on the page; and some words were becoming difficult to make out.) I reached into my dress to do the deed, but alas, I could not bring myself to.

I groaned again, louder.

'What was that, dearest?' enquired Harriet, who was sitting in the chair opposite, embroidering another cushion with the quote 'She that can heroically endure adversity will bear prosperity with equal greatness of soul.'

I shook my head and could not reply to her. The pain worsened in my stomach until I became a bit worried and thought that I might actually be ill. What if I had a fast-growing cancerous growth? It would be unfortunate, but at least I would not have to marry my cousin. Instead of preparing for our wedding in three months, he would be attending my funeral. I gave a snort of laughter, causing Harriet to frown worriedly and no doubt wonder if I were delirious.

Another two days passed in a similar manner, and the pain I was experiencing did not go away. It moved to different places in my body. Most recently, it was lodged in my side, causing a sharp pinching sting and difficulty breathing whenever I shifted position in bed or on the sofa.

With the dreary weather and my certainty that I was heading for an early grave, my mood was maudlin indeed.

On the morning of the third day, I sat silently at the breakfast table with Harriet and Papa, nibbling at a piece of buttered toast with a lacklustre appetite. I had dragged myself downstairs after a sleepless night, so I was there in body if not in spirit.

'Post for you, miss,' said Mary, handing me a couple of letters when she came to collect our plates.

'Oooh, who are they from?' asked Harriet, peering over curiously. With the rain keeping us cooped up inside, she was as bored as I was.

'One is from Jane,' I replied, recognising her elegant cursive immediately. She was probably wondering why I had not replied to her letter from last week. Little did she know I was now engaged to Mr Humbleton. I was sure she would be shocked and pity me (and probably add it as a plot point to her story). So understandably, I was reluctant to inform her of my change in circumstance. I set it aside and took up the other one. As soon as I saw the handwriting, my heart gave a quiver. But this time, he had penned it in black ink, not red crayon.

Hardly daring to breathe, I opened the flaps and found myself staring at a banknote for £10. There was a brief accompanying message, stating,

Dear Miss Blackburn,

As promised, I have sent you funds to cover any expenses incurred from my recent visit. Again, I implore your utmost discretion in this matter, for my sake as well as yours.

Yours,
M. Fitzroy

Oh! I did not want his money even if the amount was hugely generous! I wanted him to speak words of affection, for his eyes to turn heated when he looked at me and for his hands to roam again over my backside as he kissed me—I had been able to think of nothing else since it had occurred!

'Please excuse me. I need to go to my room,' I muttered and left the table, taking both letters before Harriet could ask me any further questions. Upstairs, I flung his letter and banknote into my dresser drawer and slammed it shut.

It made me feel dirty, as if he was paying me off to keep my mouth shut about his behaviour. Did he not trust me to keep quiet otherwise?

I paced around the room, wringing my hands, anger clawing at me, and thinking bad thoughts about him and what I would say to him if I ever saw him again.

But would I ever see him again? It appeared unlikely since he was now in London and apparently had no plans to return to Steventon. And I would be going to Hertfordshire in three months' time.

Finally, feeling drained, I sat on my bed and opened Jane's letter. Hopefully, she had some cheerful news to raise my spirits.

I had just broken the seal with my fingertip when there was the sound of running footsteps in the hallway, and Harriet burst in without knocking. 'Jane's here!' she exclaimed excitedly.

Hot on Harriet's heels, hair damp and cheeks flushed from the cold air, Jane entered the room, albeit more calmly, pulling off her gloves. My nerves were in tatters, and I was so relieved to see her that I immediately burst into tears, which caused no end of commotion and fuss from them both.

I was firmly embraced by Jane, who sat on the bed and kindly let me cry on her shoulder without asking questions.

'Can you fetch a handkerchief?' I heard her murmur above my head as I shook and shuddered, and the front of her dress became sodden. A clean white handkerchief was produced by Harriet, and I snuffled into it while she rubbed my back and made sympathetic noises.

Finally, my tears abated.

'I ... I was just about t-to r-read your l-letter,' I said, hiccupping.

'Never mind that,' said Jane. 'It's just an enquiry about your health and wondering why you did not reply. It isn't like you, so I decided to come over. Has something happened?'

I shook my head and could not speak.

Harriet supplied the sad news on my behalf. 'She is to be married. To Mr Humbleton.'

'What?' cried Jane, sounding horrified. 'When?'

'T-three m-months' t-time!' I wailed.

'She signed a contract to marry him,' stated Harriet matter-of-factly. 'We will go to Hertfordshire for Fliss's wedding. Then we will live there with him. Papa has given me leave to be with my sister since I will be unmarried also. There may be more chance of my meeting an eligible gentleman there than here ...' Harriet bit her lip and looked away.

'I cannot make sense of this. Fliss, why on earth would you sign your life over to him?' Jane grasped my shoulder and shook it.

'Our cousin is desperate for a wife, and there are circumstances that make it ... difficult for her to refuse him.' Harriet replied diplomatically. 'She was backed into a corner. I was there, and it was horrible. She had no choice in the matter.'

Jane made noise of disgust and released me. She got up and strode around the room, wringing her hands, like I had been doing before she arrived.

'No, no,' she muttered, almost as if to herself. 'This won't do at all. This is not what is meant to happen ...'

Harriet and I looked at each other. But I knew what Jane may have been referring to: her story, where she was obviously planning a happy ending for Elizabeth and Mr Darcy. Well, I hoped she continued writing it. *It would be nice to read about other people being happy*, I thought wistfully.

'What are your present thoughts and feelings towards Mr Fitzroy?' she asked suddenly.

I gulped and could not stop a blush from rising in my cheeks.

'I ... I may have feelings towards him, and he may have indirectly proposed ...' Harriet and Jane gasped. 'But it was a proposal that was made in jest,' I continued hastily. 'I cannot say exactly *what* happened, but I believe he has no wish to honour the engagement.'

Jane frowned, the smooth skin on her forehead wrinkling delicately. 'I did not think him the kind of man to behave so. Did he propose under some kind of delirium?'

I nodded. 'You could say that.'

She pursed her lips and looked troubled.

'What is it? Have you heard something?' I asked, a sense of dread creeping over me. *Did someone see us in the field that night? Had word been spreading around the village about Mr Fitzroy and me behaving improperly?*

'It is more gossip than anything, I fear,' said Jane in a reluctant tone. 'I was not going to say anything, but now I think I should.'

I took a deep breath and steeled myself. But what came next was not what I expected. It was worse.

'Cassie went to the post shop yesterday and overheard a maid from Ashbury Manor tell Mrs Sutton that Mr Fitzroy had taken the spare carriage and left in great haste the other morning for London looking most unlike himself. He had barely paused to eat breakfast. She believed—and this was only her opinion, mind you—that he intended to propose to Rosalind Whiteley. Mrs Sutton asked why she thought that, and the maid said he had been moping and drinking heavily since Lady Whiteley had left with Mr Pringle and that he had seemed heartsick in her absence.'

My blood went cold upon hearing this news, and I slumped against the headboard.

'What?' I whispered, my heart wrenching in extreme pain.

Jane shook her head. 'It is utter rubbish, I am sure of it. Mr Fitzroy pining over Lady Whiteley? It hardly seems possible. She is such a cold fish.'

'A cold fish that has nabbed him nonetheless,' I replied despondently as realisation set in. He had been practising his proposal to her—on me!

What a mess. Mr Fitzroy had obviously remembered enough about our interactions the next morning to be horrified at making such a mistake.

Indeed, the thought of my inferior connections and condition in life had appalled him so much that he had raced off to London to propose to Rosalind forthwith—and paid me handsomely to keep quiet.

'I suppose it does not matter what Mr Fitzroy does or whom he marries. My fate is now linked to Mr Humbleton's,' I said glumly. 'As Harriet said, we will live in Hertfordshire with him until Papa passes, and then we will return to Steventon or sell the house. It is all decided.'

'But three months is a reasonable amount of time. Something may happen to break the engagement?' suggested Jane, sounding hopeful.

'I cannot think what. I signed a contract. The only way he may break it off is if I behave so badly with another man that he is forced to. But then that would ruin my reputation and Harriet's. No one would consider marrying her, least of all ...' I did not dare say his name for fear of jinxing it. 'An amiable gentleman,' I finished, glancing at her, and Harriet let out a shuddering sigh. She was being tortured as much as I was!

'Oh, how I wish we had never set eyes on those two gentlemen and that they had stayed in London and never let Ashbury Manor!' she burst out.

Jane started pulling on her gloves determinedly.

'This is all quite awful, but do not give up, either of you. There will be a way to fix it to both your advantages. I do not quite know how yet, but hold on to hope. This is just a small setback, I assure you.'

I wanted to believe her, but she was writing a romantic story that demanded a joyful resolution. Surely, she was deluded in thinking that such things happened in real life? In real life, there was no guarantee a woman would marry the man she loved. And even if she did, she might then die from having his child. I was living proof of that!

No, being married to Mr Humbleton, along with financial security and personal freedom, could also provide me with something else—emotional safety—a condition that was looking more appealing than heartbreak.

Chapter 18

Although I managed somewhat to reconcile my mind to my future husband, my heart refused to be tamed. I knew I did not love Mr Humbleton in the slightest, and I mourned the loss of Mr Fitzroy after Jane's unwelcome news. Thinking of him wed to Rosalind, even though she was logically a better match for him, was too much to bear. I shed quiet tears alone in my room and louder, more ferocious ones when I took George out for a ride. At least the rain had eased off, allowing me to escape from the house; and if my red eyes and runny nose were commented upon when I returned, I would say I had been caught in a rogue shower. I hoped that, in time, I would come to accept my destiny and the myriad benefits that being married to Mr Humbleton offered me. But I knew I had a hard road ahead of me to reach that place.

Unfortunately, almost as if he had some uncanny foresight, my cousin sensed that I was struggling; and Papa received a lengthy letter from him not long after Jane visited. He relayed the contents to me at breakfast, and I listened with mounting horror.

'It seems Percival has arranged everything for your wedding more speedily than he thought he could. It will take place next week.'

I sucked in a sharp breath. *What?*

Papa continued reading, oblivious to my reaction. 'He has already set off and will be arriving in Steventon to collect us in two days' time. The wedding will be a small affair with just our family and a few of his good friends and neighbours ... Well, this is all happening rather fast! But I suppose it is a good thing, Felicity, as you will be settled in Hertfordshire before winter sets in,' Papa said, blinking at the letter.

'But what about a wedding dress?' I lamented. 'I haven't even picked out the material.' Understandably, I had been dragging my heels on that account!

'Ah, he has mentioned that too. Here, this bit at the end says he does not wish any fuss on that matter as he knows it is an extra expense and that any good white dress will do. He suggests you wear the one you wore to the ball at Ashbury Manor as you looked very pretty in it. It is really quite thoughtful of him.'

Harriet and I looked at each other, and my blood began to boil. Not even to have a wedding dress! Oh, he was a horrible man! And to think I had to live with him under the same roof for decades until one of us died!

How would I ever cope?

Another letter arrived from him in the afternoon post; this one was addressed to me.

My dearest cousin Felicity,

By now you should have received the news that our wedding is to be much sooner than expected and that I am travelling with haste to Steventon. All arrangements, such as they are, have been made. So there is no reason to delay. God has blessed us as there was an unexpected opening in the church schedule for next week—a bride eloped with the groom's brother, a most distasteful business. But you need not concern yourself with that!

Rest assured that you will have a few days to acquaint yourself with your surroundings and accommodation before the ceremony. I have asked the housekeeper to have all the rooms thoroughly cleaned and aired (even the rugs beaten and curtains shaken out of doors), and the small parlour downstairs is being made ready for your own particular use. It is a pretty room, with a pleasing pastel decor, a fireplace, and a view out to the garden. You must tell me what flowers are your favourites, and I will tell the gardener to plant them. I will make a note for us to discuss it in the carriage on the return journey.

Your fiancé,

P. Humbleton

I groaned inwardly and cursed the bride that had eloped with the groom's brother. If she had not, I would have had another three months of freedom. As it was, I had barely a day and a half as my fiancé was on his way! I had a vision of him yelling out the carriage window to the driver, urging him to travel at breakneck speed.

It was not like Mr Humbleton to be so reckless. Was it pre-wedding jitters brought on by the errant bride? I did not know, but something had lit a fire under his heels.

I went to bed that night feeling disgruntled and out of sorts (Sue could not even tempt me with a slice of my favourite custard tart for dessert).

Yet despite lying there for many hours, sleep evaded me. I kept thinking of Mr Fitzroy and wondering if he had proposed to Rosalind and what sort of wedding dress she would have. It would be much more extravagant than my tired muslin. There was no doubt about that.

Even though my wish for a love match has not been

fulfilled, surely, Harriet will have better luck? I thought, attempting to be philosophical. Possibly not with Mr Pringle, though, for I knew her hope of ever being engaged to him was stretching rather thin by now.

My wandering thoughts turned to the bride who had eloped with the groom's brother. She had made things difficult for me, but how positively daring and brave of her at the same time. It was obviously a love match as she would not have risked her reputation otherwise.

As I mused upon this event and my impending wedding, an idea popped into my head: *What if I ran away myself?* It was so shocking a thought that my stomach flipped, and a hot flush of excitement came over me. Surely, I would not be so bold?

But the more I chewed on it, the more it seemed like a brilliant solution. Mr Fitzroy's banknote would enable me to rent a cheap room in London for a number of months, and I could look for work or offer my services as a dressmaker. It had been some years since I had actually made a dress, and my skills were rusty. But Papa had taught both Harriet and me, so we had the knowledge. A solid plan started to take shape—I could send for Harriet when I was set up, and we could start our own business as her dressmaking skills were far superior than mine! Of course we could not tell Papa because he would come and get us immediately. But I could send word to him via Jane that we were safe and well. And she and Cassie could even come and visit us if they wished. It would be a hard life, and we might be poor, but we would be free and independent of any man.

It was certainly better than being married to someone I did not love and sitting in a small parlour looking out the window for the rest of my life. How boring was that! My idea was risky, but a much more thrilling way to live.

But if I was to do it, it had to be now as it would be light shortly; and if Mr Humbleton was 'travelling with haste', he could arrive at any moment. If so, I would have no chance of escape. Throwing back the covers, I got out of bed, lit a candle, and dressed quickly in my warmest dress and coat. Plucking the rest of my day dresses from the wardrobe, along with all my petticoats and chemises, I thrust them into a canvas bag and added wool stockings, gloves, my best bonnet, and a scarf. In my reticule, I placed a comb, a few pieces of jewellery, and, most importantly, Mr Fitzroy's banknote. I left my hair in its bedtime plait as I did not have time to fuss with it.

Slinging my (now rather heavy) bundle over my shoulder, I took the candle, inched open the door of my room, and slipped out. Stealing along the corridor, I hesitated outside Harriet's room. The chance of her trying to stop me was great, but I could not leave without telling her what I was doing. Besides, as I did not have time to write a note to Papa, she would have to be the messenger.

I stood by her bed and looked down at her sleeping form. 'Harriet dearest,' I whispered. 'Wake up.'

Harriet stirred and groggily opened her eyes. Then as her gaze focused and landed on my bundle, she sat up abruptly, now fully awake.

'Fliss, what on earth ...?'

'Shhh,' I said, sitting on the side of the bed. 'Just listen, for I do not have much time.'

Quickly, I outlined my plan, telling her that George and I would ride to London—it should take three days at most—and that we would stay at inns along the way. And that I had a little money so I could rent a room when I reached London and I would look for seamstress work.

To give her credit, Harriet did not immediately protest but listened quietly. Encouraged, I went on.

'When I have set myself up, I will send word, and you can come and visit me or live in London too permanently. It will be difficult, but we must be brave and depend on ourselves for once. I am determined to prove that a woman does not need a man to survive.'

Harriet shuddered and glanced at *Fanny Hill* on her bedside table.

'And I forbid you to read that book while I am gone. I promise you I will not end up like Fanny. Can you please just let Papa know? Sorry to give you the job of being the bearer of bad news.'

'All right,' said Harriet smoothly. 'I will tell him in the morning. He will be upset, and our cousin will be livid, but he has no one to blame but himself.'

I was shocked that she was so agreeable to my idea. 'You are not going to stop me?'

She shook her head. 'I can see you are determined, and it is mostly a foolproof plan.'

'Mostly?'

'Yes. Well, George may refuse to travel that far, and you could get stranded halfway to London. Or you might get robbed and freeze to death by the roadside. If you do make it, there is the poverty you will no doubt face in London when your money runs out if you cannot get work. You may indeed end up selling your body on the street so you can buy a loaf of bread. Despite all that, I think it is a solid alternative to a loveless marriage.'

I gulped. But it was too late to back out now—I had made up my mind.

George was most surprised at being woken at such an early hour but happily munched on a nosebag of oats while I saddled him up.

Dawn was breaking when—after my own hasty breakfast of yesterday's rolls, butter, and honey—I led him out of the stable and mounted. By my reckoning, we would reach Reading in four to five hours, including pauses to drink from streams and for George to eat some more oats. At Reading, we would stop for the night, and I would take a room at a roadside inn so I could eat a decent meal and George could bed down in their stable.

Depending on the weather and how George was feeling, we would continue on to Maidenhead the next day and then reach the outskirts of London the day after that. The roads would be muddy from the rain, so I would have to pay close attention to where George was stepping so he did not slip over. But at least the morning sky was showing streaks of blue and rose rather than the uniform grey of the past week, and I was hopeful for some sunshine along the way. This was going to be the longest ride of my life, but even with all the risks involved, I was determined to embrace my freedom.

After a long glance at my silent house, I clicked to George, and we set off up the lane at a slow trot. Despite setting out with reasonably high spirits, after ten minutes, I was missing Harriet; and after twenty minutes, I was regretting my hasty decision to leave. The road was not in too bad a condition, but it seemed never-ending, and I was already getting saddle sore. My bundle of clothing, which I had slung over my neck and rested on the pommel, kept sliding off and nearly choking me. George had also started fussing with his bit, which was irritating. 'George, stop it!' I tapped him with the end of the reins, but he chose not to respond and continued jerking his head.

This would not do; we were barely half an hour into the journey, and there were many hours and days to go. *Perhaps I should have taken the buggy*, I thought. *At least it would have been more comfortable.*

I was pondering this when a thunderous gallop was heard approaching from up ahead. Someone was in a hurry. It was probably just a mail messenger, but in case it was Mr Humbleton, I decided it would be best to leave the path and head into an adjoining field and hide behind a thicket of trees. Of course, George chose this moment to misbehave and would not move because he liked being on the drier path, and the field was waterlogged. He planted his hooves and refused to budge an inch, no matter how much I kicked my heels.

In desperation, I gave him a slap on the rump and screeched at him, and he grudgingly walked off the path into the field and picked his way over the boggy ground to the trees. If he could talk, I knew he would be cursing me.

But at this point, my escape was more important than him having clean hooves!

By this time, the rider was all but upon us, and I attempted to coerce George to move faster. But it was too late—there came a faint 'Whoa, boy', and I knew we had been seen. There was silence; then the sound of squelching came to my ears as the rider started to follow me into the field on their horse. *Blast!* I did not turn around. If it was Mr Humbleton, he may not have recognised me yet. But the squelching increased in pace, and panicking, I kicked George into a fast trot and then a canter. He resisted at first but then thankfully, for whatever reason, decided to acquiesce; and we took off across the field, mud and water spraying up behind us. My aim was to rejoin the path ahead and neatly evade the rider, but it was lined for quite a way by a tall hedge, so I could do nothing but urge George ever onwards. To my dismay, I heard a snort from behind, and then the rider began cantering too and encroaching; whoever they were, their horse's speed was much superior to mine!

A deep male voice cried out behind me, 'Halt, Miss Blackburn!'

Damn and double blast!

'Faster, George!' I cried, spurring him into a gallop, determined not to let Mr Humbleton catch me.

'Felicity! Stop!'

A jolt went through me. Oh, that was not Mr Humbleton's voice; it was another infinitely more dear! I turned in the saddle to check, but at that moment, another event occurred. A brown rabbit had decided to seek drier ground, and it hopped across the field right in front of George. He reared up in a panic, and I screamed and clung on to his neck. That may have been the end of the matter. But when he came down, he planted his forefeet on the ground and threw his hindquarters into the air, effectively bucking me off. Sailing in slow motion over his head, my life briefly flashed before my eyes before I landed with a resounding splash on my back in a large puddle of muddy water.

Chapter 19

I lay there, stunned, until a figure loomed over me; and I found myself staring up into a pair of startling blue eyes, not dissimilar to the colour of the cloudless sky beyond the gentleman's head.

'Do not move!' commanded Mr Fitzroy, his dark hair tousled from the wild ride and his expression grave with concern.

I could not move even if I had wanted to—the air had been punched clean out of my lungs. All I could do was stare at him wide-eyed as I attempted to draw in ragged breaths, but it became easier to do so after a few minutes.

'Can you speak?' he asked.

I opened my mouth and uttered an 'arrrrggh'.

He smiled. 'Good, you have been winded a little, but you can make some noise at least. Now, forgive me, but I must ascertain if you have any injuries.'

Gently, he started prodding at my ankles and then moved slowly up my legs, asking 'Does this hurt?' at intervals, while I croaked out 'no' or 'a little', depending on the pressure of the prodding. Eventually, he felt around my midriff and proceeded to prod at the soft area underneath my breasts. I gasped as his hands then moved upward.

'Mr Fitzroy!' I wheezed.

'I need to be sure you have not broken any ribs,' he murmured, continuing his slow inspection.

'I do not think my ribs are that high up!' I exclaimed, suddenly regaining my powers of speech. I batted his hands away from my bosom, and he sat back on his heels and assisted me as I struggled to sit up.

'Careful,' he said.

'Thank you, I believe I am all right.' Indeed, I could breathe freely and wiggle my toes and fingers; and although my spine felt bruised, I would live—no thanks to George, who was calmly standing nearby as if nothing had happened. Mr Fitzroy's big black horse had wandered over to join him, and the two were whickering together as if sharing a private joke.

'You were lucky,' Mr Fitzroy continued. 'Your luggage seems to have cushioned the worst of the blow.'

'My luggage?'

He reached behind and drew out my now-flat bundle of dresses, petticoats, and other accessories. It seemed to have slipped behind me as I was airborne and acted as a mattress when I came down. It was fortunate that I had not packed too lightly!

'Do you want to tell me what you are doing here?' he asked.

'What *I* am doing?' I echoed, ignoring his question. 'What are *you* doing here? You are meant to be in London.'

'As you can see, I am not. I received some harrowing news. I set off immediately, and I have been riding all night.' He passed a hand over his tired stubbled face, and looking more closely at his rumpled appearance, I could believe it.

'What news was so important?'

Mr Fitzroy grasped my hand. 'That you are engaged to your cousin, of course! Tell me it is not true.'

I wondered how he had found out. Mr Humbleton, in his glee, must have mentioned it to the postmistress before he had left; and the word had spread like wildfire—to London no less!

I could not meet his eyes. 'It is true. I ... I signed a contract. Papa negotiated the terms, and it was in my best interest to do so.'

To my surprise, Mr Fitzroy dropped my hand and swore loudly.

'It was *not* in your best interest nor mine!' he said angrily. 'Forgive me, but I seem to recall quite clearly that I proposed to *you*, and *you* accepted me. And now I find out that you have accepted another man's offer!'

His mouth pressed into a straight line, and his black

brows drew together, and he looked altogether menacing. It annoyed me immensely. *How dare he get so angry when he had done nothing but send me a banknote? And run off to propose to someone else!*

'Forgive *me* for saying so, sir, but you were not in your right mind that night. And the letter you left behind made it sound like you were berating yourself in the cold light of day for having proposed. Besides, what is it to you if I am engaged to him?' I exclaimed, feeling unjustly accused when he was no longer on the market himself. 'Are you not recently engaged to Lady Whiteley?'

Mr Fitzroy stared at me. 'Lady Whiteley?' he repeated, sounding confused.

'Yes, you rode off to London forthwith after you had practised your drunken proposal to her upon me!'

He sighed and took up my hand again. 'Felicity, I was drunk because I was terrified about proposing. The delivery did not go quite as planned. But I assure you, the intention was there, however slurred my speech and idiotic my behaviour may have been to make you believe otherwise. I rode to London in haste to consult with my lawyer to ensure that the matter between us was indeed legal. I did not want you to be compromised. He has assured me it is. But now with this contract you have signed with your cousin ...' He ran his free hand through his hair and glowered at me.

It was my turn to be confused after hearing all this.

'Mr Fitzroy, you are making little sense. Please speak plainly. So you are you saying you were not just practising on me for Lady Whiteley?'

He swore again. 'No! Dammit, Felicity! I love *you*! I have been half crazed with longing ever since we first met at the assembly. And then at the lake, I fell even harder, though I could not admit it to myself. At the ball, I tried to convey how I felt, and I thought when I came to call, I thought ... I hoped that it would make it very clear! I am besotted—' He stopped, blushing profusely.

I stared at him, hardly daring to believe my ears. 'You love me?'

He nodded. 'Most ardently.'

My heart melted like butter on warm bread, and I squeezed his hand hard. 'I love you too.'

Mr Fitzroy let out a sigh of relief and bent his forehead to my own. 'Thank the Lord for that,' he breathed.

'And you are definitely *not* engaged to Lady Whiteley?' I asked just to make sure.

His head shot up, and our eyes locked. 'Indeed I am not! How could I ever be engaged to her when all I can think of is you?'

A strange feeling of utter despair and intense pleasure stole over me all at once—utter despair that I was now engaged to Mr Humbleton and intense pleasure that Mr Fitzroy loved me. But still, I could not let him off the hook that easily.

'But at the assembly, you told Mr Pringle that you thought the Austens' piglets were more attractive!'

Max threw back his head and laughed uproariously. 'You heard that?'

'Yes, Jane and I were outside getting some air. It was why I initially disliked you,' I said, wondering why he thought such an insulting statement was so funny.

'Oh dear, I do apologise. I did not realise anyone else was listening. It was false, of course. I had to tell Evan that so he didn't suspect anything. If he had known what I really thought ... Well, as you may have assessed by now, I am an extremely private person.'

'So what did you *really* think, if I may ask? As my feelings were rather hurt by it.'

Max stared at me intently, his blue eyes seeming to bore into my soul. 'Very well, if you wish to know. I thought that you were the most beautiful girl I had ever seen, and I could not take my eyes off you.'

'Go on,' I said. 'What else?'

He swallowed. 'Uh, when we met unexpectedly in Overton, I was elated. As I was desperate to spend more time with you, I jumped at the chance to offer you and your sister a ride home. The carriage ride was too short, and you seemed upset with me and we clashed again at the lake, and I was in agony about what to do until your letter of apology arrived. Then at the ball, I could hardly believe you agreed to dance with me. I was in heaven until Rosalind commandeered me for the rest of the evening, and I could not rid myself of her. I called at your house with the intention of courting you. But your cousin, I suspect, saw that and tried to put me off. And then the cake incident happened ...'

I giggled, and his full lips curved into a smile.

'Yes, that was amusing. However, I was unsure of how to proceed if you really were to marry your cousin. Then when I saw you at Ashbury and you said you did not want to marry him, my feelings were such that I had to propose despite having no idea if you shared those feelings. Unfortunately, my "one stiff drink" for Dutch courage turned into several, plus a couple of bottles of wine ... I am so sorry, Felicity. Can you forgive me for making a hash of it?'

He looked so handsome and sorrowful that my heart melted all over again, and I forgave him completely, even though it had been an utter shambles.

'Of course I forgive you,' I said, inclining my head towards him.

'But perhaps you could kiss me now and stop talking?'

'Gladly,' Max said, looking relieved. 'For I have been rattling on like a nonsensical fool.'

He gathered me into his arms and placed a soft kiss on my mouth, and I kissed him back; and soon, we were caught up in a flurry of tongues and passion, lost in each other, with no thought as to who might come past and see.

Eventually, the cold muddy water seeping through my dress became too uncomfortable to ignore, and the morning was getting on. But still, we did not move from our spot in the field; it was as if we did not want to break the spell (or, more likely, the heavenly kissing to end!).

'You never answered my question. What are you doing here?' he asked curiously as he gently caressed my cheekbone, and I twined my fingers through his hair.

'Er, I was running away to London with your money to be a dressmaker.' To be honest, I had forgotten about that plan as soon as Mr Fitzroy had confessed his love for me. However, I did still think it was the right thing to do under the circumstances.

'Oh, how long do you think that would have lasted?'

'I am not sure. I may have had to sell my body on the street.'

'Any man who lays a finger on you can consider himself dead!' he growled, shoulders stiffening and eyes flashing.

I giggled.

'Mr Fitzroy, I do believe you have a jealous streak.'

He kissed me hard on the mouth, and I squeaked.

'I assure you my bark is worse than my bite, as you will find out if you still want to marry me. And please, do call me Max. I think with our newfound intimacy, we can drop the formalities.'

I chewed on my bottom lip, which indeed was feeling a bit bruised after his abundant kisses. 'All right ... Max ... And yes, I do still want to marry you. But you are forgetting there is the small problem of my legally binding engagement to Mr Humbleton. He is on his way to Steventon as we speak to collect me for the wedding.'

Max got to his feet, raised an eyebrow at the ruined state of yet another pair of his trousers, and reached down his hand to help me up. 'Then we should go and elucidate your cousin on our relationship once and for all. I am sure he will give up immediately once he hears that we love each other.'

'I hope you are right,' I said uneasily.

From what I had seen already, Mr Humbleton was not the sort of man to give up when he wanted something.

Max introduced me to his horse, who he said was called Apollo. I patted his neck, feeling a little afraid as he was huge. George was like a pony in comparison. No wonder Max had been able to travel so fast from London.

But Apollo seemed to have a gentle nature and happily accepted one of the carrots that I had brought along for George and stood quietly crunching it.

George was not as well behaved, however, and led Max on a merry chase around the field until I yelled at him (George, not Max) to stop playing and get over here at once. Then he allowed Max to catch him and tether him to Apollo.

Max shook his head at me. 'Your horse needs obedience training.'

I sighed. 'I know, he is very naughty.'

'Maybe I can help with that.'

I nodded and hid a smile, imagining Max attempting to school George and tearing his hair out in frustration.

'Right up you get.' He grasped me around the waist and lifted me up onto Apollo's saddle with ease. I blinked, remembering how muscular his arms were at the lake. Those strong arms now encircled my body protectively; as he mounted, he settled himself behind me and took up the reins.

We set off at a reasonably paced trot back to Steventon with George pulling occasionally, unused to being tethered.

I did not say much, content to lie back against Max's warm broad chest and listen to him humming a little ditty above my head (it was the same one he had been singing drunkenly in the field). But after a mile or so, my back started to ache, and the jarring motion of riding was not helping. I shifted slightly, attempting to get comfortable.

'Are you sore?' Max asked.

I nodded.

'We will be there soon, and then you can rest.'

He kissed my temple and murmured an endearment. Tears sprang into my eyes as tender feelings flooded my chest. 'No matter what happens, I love you,' I blurted, unable to prevent the words from tumbling forth.

'I love you too,' Max said immediately. 'But you need not worry. I am not going to lose you when we have just found each other.'

I took a deep breath, knowing that the subject was going to come up at some point, so it may as well be now before he found himself trapped. 'There is something I have to say that may change your mind about marrying me.'

I felt the muscles in his arms tighten. 'There is nothing you could say that will make me change my mind.' But I detected an edge of wariness in his voice.

This might, I thought, steeling myself to say the words.

I took a deep breath. 'Max, I'm sorry, but I don't want children or even one child, to be honest.'

There was a long silence, which was punctuated by a snuffling noise from George.

'Is there a reason why?' Max asked eventually. To my relief, he did not sound offended, only curious.

Stiltedly, I relayed the sorry tale of my mother dying at my birth and my fear of the same thing happening to me.

'Ah, I see. So you are not against the marriage act itself, but afraid of the consequences of it?'

I nodded.

'For there is nothing to fear regarding the former, I assure you, and I would take care to be gentle the first time.'

I nodded again, blushing, but did not say anything. Little did he know that I was not as inexperienced as he assumed! But to all intents and purposes, I was still a virgin.

Max cleared his throat above me. 'A-as for the other, there is s-something called a French letter. Men w-wear it on their you-know-whats, and it p-prevents b-b-babies.'

I could tell by the stuttering it took to get these words out that he was highly embarrassed to have this conversation. But I felt nothing but relief to talk about it.

'You would do that for me?'

He shrugged. 'Of course. I'm not sure I want children either. I don't know if I would be a good father after not having had much to do with my own.'

I patted his thigh. 'I am sure you would be,' I said reassuringly. I had a sudden image of him lifting a child joyfully into the air and kissing them and felt bad that he would never get the chance to do so.

'But it is your choice, Felicity,' he continued. 'I would never force motherhood upon you if you did not want it. But if you perhaps changed your mind ... in the future ... then we would discuss it, and I would seek the services of the best doctor and midwife in the country. I would do everything I could to make sure nothing happened to you.'

'I know, but even then, you cannot control the outcome. I am sure Papa took great care of Mama, but she still died,' I said. 'But I appreciate the sentiment, and thank you for talking so openly about it.'

Max kissed the top of my head, and we fell into a comfortable silence until we reached Steventon, each thinking our own thoughts about how our shared future might play out with this new revelation.

I prayed fervently that my choosing to speak to him about my unconventional decision to remain childless would not come to divide us at a later point. But I knew—and I was sure Jane would agree with me on this—honesty was always the best policy in matters of the heart.

Chapter 20

'No no no, this is preposterous! I do not believe it!' exclaimed Mr Humbleton, striding backwards and forwards with an agitated look on his face.

'But 'tis true! Max proposed to me, and I accepted him,' I repeated firmly. 'I did not say anything previously because I believed him to be ... fooling around, but he was not.' I thought it wise to skip over the fact that Max had been blind drunk at the time!

Mr Humbleton did not look impressed. 'Cousin, may I remind you, you signed a contract to marry *me*. And it is legally binding. I have it right here.'

He pulled the document out of his breast pocket with a flourish, and I felt sick. As I suspected, he was not going to let me go without a jolly good fight.

Max and I had arrived back at the house, muddy and exhausted, to find it in an uproar, thanks to Harriet spilling the beans at breakfast that I had run away to London rather than marry a man I did not love.

She told me that Papa had been so distraught at the news that he had shouted at her in the most alarming manner.

Frightened, she had burst into tears, ran upstairs, and locked herself in her room. Aunt had been hastily sent for and, with Mary's help, had coaxed her out. Next, Mr Humbleton had arrived to find his bride-to-be missing and had exploded in fury.

Now we were all ensconced in the parlour, facing his wrath. Max and I stood before him like we were in the dock. Thankfully, Max had his arm around me, for I was so tired I felt I might sink to the floor and never get up. Yet I knew I had to endure this horridness in order to free myself.

'You, sir, have stolen my fiancée. And I demand you release her to me at once!' spat Mr Humbleton, pointing an accusing finger at Max.

'She is not your property, but a grown woman with her own free will,' Max said in a calm voice. 'And Felicity chooses to be with me. Don't you, my dear?'

'I do indeed,' I said solemnly. 'Of my own free will,' I added in case that bit was needed. I glanced at Harriet sitting with Aunt on the sofa, and she clasped her hands to her bosom and gave me a sweet encouraging smile.

'But all the arrangements have been made for us to marry,' said Mr Humbleton, faltering.

'Be that as it may,' said Max steadily. 'But they can just as easily be unmade. Besides, if my understanding of the events is correct, I think you will find that I proposed the night before she signed your contract. So *I* am actually her fiancé, not you.'

He looked down at me for support, and I agreed that was indeed true. *Yes, point to Max!*

But my cousin rallied and came back with a riposte of his own.

'Do you have proof?' asked Mr Humbleton.

'Proof?' echoed Max.

'Yes, man, proof! I assume your proposal was done in haste. Who is to say it did not happen today when you accosted her on the road to London with only field mice as onlookers? You will need solid proof or at least a witness who can testify in court that your proposal came before mine.' He smiled at us smugly, and I could tell he was deadly serious about taking the matter to court. I gazed up at Max, who was looking worried.

'I have no witness apart from Felicity,' he said slowly.

'Well, her testimony is no good since she has already signed my contract. Have you none other?'

'I ... I told Jane and Harriet,' I said. 'But that was after I signed the contract.'

Mr Humbleton shrugged. 'Then it is settled. There is no engagement between the two of you, and the contract with me still stands. Cousin, if you would be so kind as to clean and tidy yourself.' He looked with distaste at my mud-caked dress and rampant hair. 'We will be leaving in an hour!'

Everyone looked a bit shocked, and Aunt clicked her tongue at his belligerent tone.

'Max!' I uttered, clutching his arm, feeling faint with despair (and hunger since I had not eaten anything but a roll and honey since early this morning). The thought of being parted from him and being stuck in a carriage with Mr Humbleton for many hours as we rolled towards Hertfordshire was agonising.

'She is not going anywhere with you! She needs a decent meal and to rest properly!' Max growled at Mr Humbleton. 'You cannot just lug her off to wherever it is you are from!'

'Hertfordshire,' said Mr Humbleton proudly. 'A small, but picturesque village with a lovely aspect—'

'I don't care what it looks like!' Max cried, his face red and his fists clenched; I could practically see steam coming out of his ears.

Papa stood up then and intervened, seeing as things were getting ugly.

'Felicity shall eat and rest and be ready in three hours,' he said. 'Harriet and her aunt can help her pack.'

My cousin considered and nodded. 'Very well. We should still reach Reading by nightfall.'

I groaned inwardly. I was to go back the way I had just come! Mr Humbleton must have passed by Max and me in his carriage while we were sitting in that muddy field behind the hedge. We had been so caught up in canoodling we had not heard a thing.

Prompted by Papa gesturing to her, Harriet came over and held out her hand to me. 'Come, dearest,' she said, sounding pained. 'Let us get you cleaned up and fed. All will be well.'

I was not so sure of that, but what else could I do? Mr Humbleton seemed to hold all the cards.

Max watched helplessly as I was extracted from him and led towards the door. But just as Harriet and I were about to exit, he shouted, 'Wait! What is that?' He was pointing at me.

Perplexed, I looked down at my person to see what he was pointing at but could not determine what it was.

He strode over on his long legs and plucked something from my sleeve. 'This! I recognise it.'

It took me a few seconds to know what he was referring to; then I realised.

'Oh, yes, it is the letter you wrote me,' I said. 'I had placed it in the bosom of my dress for safe keeping. It must have lodged in my sleeve when I fell off George.'

'You fell off George?' said Harriet, aghast. 'Are you all right?'

'Yes, I think so, just a bit of a sore back …'

'You can tell her later,' said Max, interrupting excitedly. 'For I think this letter is enough proof to show that I proposed first.'

I snapped my fingers. 'Of course! You signed and dated it, ever the consummate gentleman, even when you are hungover.'

Max bowed to me with a grin. 'My lady. The honour should go to you, though, as you actually kept the letter instead of tearing it up as I so rightly deserved.'

'Well, you wrote it,' I said shyly. 'Of course I was going to keep it.'

Max took my hand and kissed it, and we smiled at each other fondly.

'Not so soon with the lovey-dovey twaddle. Let me see that!' Mr Humbleton sneered. He snatched the paper out of Max's hand and perused it intently.

'It is written in crayon, not ink. It does not count!' he cried triumphantly.

'Sir, I think you'll find if you look in any dictionary that a crayon is a writing and drawing implement, so it does indeed count,' said Max. 'It states plainly that I proposed to Felicity and she accepted the day before she signed your contract. You can have your lawyer check the document if you like, but I think you'll find that mine will stand before a judge and jury. Any claim you have on her is now null and void. Besides, Felicity and I have done more than just kiss, so she is compromised—and we have to marry,' he added.

Harriet stared at me, shocked, and Aunt shook her head and said, 'Oh dear.' I did not think Max massaging my buttocks was tantamount to being 'compromised', but I hung my head in mock shame and let them think what they liked.

By the look of pure rage on Mr Humbleton's face, it was the icing on the cake.

'What?' he roared. 'I have no wish to be married to such a ... a strumpet!'

'Good!' I retorted, not caring what he thought of me. 'For I have no wish to be married to you either. I am sorry for your predicament, but I am not the one to solve it and bid you leave and look elsewhere for a wife.'

Mr Humbleton muttered something about not wanting the good folk of Hertfordshire to be polluted by the likes of me anyway.

'But, Felicity!' cried Papa. 'Are you sure you want to be married to Mr Fitzroy? I did not think you liked him.'

'I do like him, Papa. Very much so. In fact, I ... I love him, and he loves me.'

Max nodded, looking a touch embarrassed to be sharing such intimate feelings with my family.

'Well then', said Papa with a wide smile and an

undisguised look of relief, 'I offer you both my blessing and my hearty congratulations.' He came over and shook Max's hand.

'And mine too. Congratulations,' said Aunt and gave a low curtsy to Max and me as if we were the king and queen, which made me giggle.

Harriet clapped her hands in glee and gave me a hug. 'Can I be your bridesmaid? Or will you have Jane?'

'I'll have you both,' I said with a laugh. 'And definitely a wedding dress!'

During this happy exchange, Mr Humbleton melted away out of the parlour without congratulating us or saying goodbye. But no one was really sorry to see him go, least of all me. I was much too busy gazing adoringly at my tall, dark, and handsome fiancé.

Soon afterwards, Max took me aside and said that he would leave for Ashbury as he needed to feed and water Apollo. 'But I will call on you this evening, if that is all right?'

I nodded. 'Yes, I believe Papa is planning an impromptu engagement party and inviting the Austens to celebrate with us.'

Max winced. 'I will have to put on my socialising face then.' He arranged his features into his trademark haughty expression, and I could not help but giggle.

'Dearest, I think that may scare them off!'

Max chuckled too. 'You may be right. Well, until then, my love.' He took my hand and kissed it, and we gazed at each other for a moment. 'I do not want to let you out of my sight,' he murmured, holding on to my hand.

'Nor I you.' I sighed with pleasure as his fingers entwined with mine, but it soon turned into a smothered yawn. He released me, telling me to go and rest immediately.

'Not that you need any beauty sleep,' he added with a wink, and I blushed. Max Fitzroy becoming adept at flirting? Wonders would never cease!

Some hours later, after a sound nap and a thorough wash, I slipped into a clean chemise and my green evening dress. Harriet curled and pinned my hair, and I fastened a simple emerald necklace that had been my mother's around my neck. I caught Harriet's eye in the mirror, and she smiled at me, tucking a stray strand of hair into place.

'You are glowing, dearest. I think being engaged to the right man agrees with you.'

It was true. I felt lit within, as if my soul might float through the window and into the dusk-filled sky. My heart danced with joy at the thought of seeing Max again shortly and even more so to be married to him in the near future!

'Oh, Harriet, I am so happy that everything has turned

out for the best. To think that Max had no intention of ever proposing to Rosalind Whiteley and that I was the object of his desire all along!'

Harriet placed a warm hand on my shoulder and grasped it firmly. 'Of course, even though she would have you think otherwise. He loves you very much. I caught him looking at you earlier with the most drippy expression.'

I giggled. 'I am sure mine was drippy too. I cannot help it. Underneath that stern facade is a sweet and kind man. Evan was right about him ...'

Harriet smiled, but I saw a glimmer of sadness in her expression at the mention of a certain gentleman's name.

I reached up and touched her hand. 'Everything will turn out right for you too. It must!'

'Evan's intention to write to me daily started off strong, but his letters have all but dried up,' she said quietly. 'I have not heard from him for nearly a week now. But I am sure he must be busy. After all, London is so diverting with its many social events, and he will have other ladies to attend to.' She let out a tiny sob, and my heart constricted.

'Harriet ...'

She swiped at her eyes and pulled herself together. 'Do not mind me, Fliss. This is *your* happy occasion, and you deserve it. You have been to hell and back with all that business with our cousin, and it has been resolved in such a perfectly wonderful way.' She smiled stoically and lifted her chin. 'I will meet you downstairs shortly, where I will be pouring you *and myself* a large congratulatory glass of Madeira!'

I laughed. 'All right!'

When she had left, I sat there a little longer, staring at the elegant young woman in the mirror, with her flushed happy cheeks and shining eyes. I touched my necklace gently.

You would like him, Mama. He is handsome, strong, funny, and very kind. And I love him so much. I wish you were here so you could celebrate with us.

Feeling like I might start sobbing myself, I quickly swiped under my eyes and gave my appearance one last check. This was not the time for wistful tears. I had a fiancé and an engagement party awaiting me downstairs!

* * *

When I walked into the parlour, Harriet cried out, 'Here she is!'

Immediately, I was embraced; and my cheeks were kissed by Jane, Cassie, and Mrs Austen with excited congratulations offered. Mr Austen bowed and offered his too. But he stood to the side with Papa, drinking port, and left it up to his women to make a fuss of me.

'We will talk properly soon,' muttered Jane in my ear and sidled off to the pianoforte, where she began to softly play a classical piece. Meanwhile, Harriet poured glasses of Madeira, and Cassie passed around a plate of cakes that Sue had hastily baked for the occasion.

Max had been hovering in the background, but he came over when the initial flurry had subsided and handed me the glass of Madeira he had fetched. He looked resplendent in a black tailcoat, cream double-breasted waistcoat, and a snowy-white cravat. Knowing that everyone was watching, he bowed formally to me. 'Good evening, Miss Blackburn.'

'Good evening, Mr Fitzroy,' I replied with a smile returning his bow.

'I remember that dress from the assembly,' he said. 'You look as lovely in it now as you did then—and bear no resemblance whatsoever to a piglet,' he added in a low voice, and I smothered a snort of laughter.

'You look rather dashing yourself, I have to say, now that you have cleaned up.'

He chuckled. 'Yes, I came over in the carriage to avoid any further mud baths.'

We exchanged a knowing smile.

To my huge relief, Max was mild in temperament and at ease with me. I was anxious after my confession about not wanting children, that he may have thought about it and

275

decided it was reprehensible. I had half expected a brief letter to be delivered outlining his change of heart and asking to break off the engagement.

But no. I could see by his deference and his smiling glances that he still liked me extremely and that I need not worry about his feelings cooling. In fact, his relaxed manner encouraged my own feelings to solidify further, and I felt a deep abiding trust starting to grow for him.

But we could not discuss anything remotely resembling our feelings at the present moment. That would have to wait.

'I see Mrs Snelling has just arrived and wishes to speak to you. I shall make myself scarce for the meanwhile.' Max bent to kiss my hand, his lips grazing the back of it. When he straightened, I saw that his look of frustration reflected my own wishes—to spend the evening alone together, to talk or kiss or whatever else we liked to do ... My pulse rate increased as he ran a finger delicately over the inside of my wrist, and I shivered—whatever else indeed! But propriety dictated that we could not be in the same room without a chaperone until we were married.

I sipped my wine and observed his well-built physique as he strolled away to talk to Papa and Mr Austen, my hand tingling from the touch of his lips. A scandalous thought about having a midnight tryst entered my mind.

Would he be shocked? Or willing? After our rendezvous in the kitchen and the heated bout of kissing in the field this morning, I had a feeling he might be entirely amenable.

'Congratulations, Felicity!' Aunt swooped in and kissed me soundly on the cheek, her lips cold after the short walk from next door. 'Well done, my dear! What an achievement!'

'Ah, thank you?' I said, not quite sure what she was getting at.

She leaned in and said in a low voice, 'You have hooked one of the most eligible bachelors in the country, my dear. He is a much better catch than that clergyman cousin of yours.'

'I would not use the word "hooked", Aunt. It was more that we finally realised our feelings for each other,' I replied, glancing quickly over at Max to make sure he was not hearing this exchange. He was now over by the piano with Jane, thank goodness!

But Aunt had more to say on the matter. She began to unpin her best hat, which had a peacock feather in it. 'He has kept this quiet since he has been in Steventon, but I have heard it from good authority that Mr Fitzroy owns a very grand house. Well, actually ... it is more of an estate ... in Derbyshire—the Peak District to be exact. It is being refurbished, hence why he was lodging with Mr Pringle for the summer. Apparently, it even has a private lake full of fish!'

Max owned an estate and a lake! Gracious, he was a private person indeed as he hadn't once mentioned it in any of our conversations. And I had been so caught up in our getting engaged today that I had not given any thought to where we would live. It appeared we had much to discuss!

Max, who was now chatting with the Austens, caught my eye as I looked over at him; and he raised his glass to me. I narrowed my eyes at the wine, and he grinned mischievously. Hopefully, he would not partake of too much and need to spend the night on the parlour couch again!

It was not until a little later that Jane and I managed to speak together. We sat on the sofa with cups of tea and helped ourselves to the second round of refreshments that Mary brought in.

'These are quite delicious,' said Jane, biting into an iced cake. 'What are they?'

'I gave our cook one of the petits fours I swiped from Rosalind Whiteley's tea party. She has successfully replicated them, albeit larger versions. They are *grande fours.*'

Jane giggled. 'But more satisfying if you are hungry.'

'Exactly.'

'So your cousin has left then, I take it?'

'Yes, in a most foul temper after he realised his fiancée now belonged to another. Papa ripped up the contract himself and apologised most profusely for ever subjecting me to him. Of course I forgave him as he was ultimately trying to do the right thing.'

'Ah, excellent news.' Jane ducked her head, and I saw that she was smirking to herself.

'What are you smiling about?' I asked.

'Nothing.' But her smirk deepened.

'Pray, do tell, Miss Austen. My suspicions are roused.'

She sighed. 'Oh, very well. I was not going to say anything, but I cannot keep it a secret from *you*. I may have written anonymously to Mr Humbleton and emotionally blackmailed him.'

I stared at her, feeling a bit shocked. 'Jane! Whatever did you say?'

She shrugged. 'Just that you had a more desirable suitor and that he needed to break off the engagement immediately, or God would not look favourably upon a man who thwarted a couple truly in love.'

'But it only made him try to marry me faster!'

'Yes, that did not quite go as I expected,' said Jane, looking sheepish. 'I hoped he would see reason, but in truth, he is an unreasonable sort of person. I also did not expect you to run away, but it was a good thing you did as you met Mr Fitzroy coming back from London. So that all worked out ...'

I suddenly had a thought as to why Max was in such a hurry to return. 'You didn't write anonymously to Mr Fitzroy as well, did you?'

Jane averted her eyes and played with a few crumbs on her plate. 'Um, perhaps ...'

I let out a breath.

'You had better tell me exactly what you said to him,' I scolded lightly.

Jane huffed. 'Only what he needed to hear. That you had been forced into an engagement with Mr Humbleton and that he needed to make haste to Steventon immediately if he didn't want to lose you forever. I thought that would put the wind up him, and I was right—it did!'

'So, really, I should be thanking you,' I said slowly. 'If you had not written to Max ...'

Jane grasped my hand. 'Flissy, I hardly did anything. I simply encouraged what was already there, and fate did the rest. You were meant to be together.'

Whether it was fate or her quill, I would probably never know as the subject was promptly dropped due to a commotion outside in the hallway.

The parlour door was suddenly flung open, and Mr Pringle burst into the room, his face pale and stricken. From the stained and rumpled state of his dress, it seemed he had been travelling for days.

'Forgive me, I came as fast as I could!' he blurted. 'My cousin bade me to go with her to Bath. But when the news came ... I left immediately, and the roads were horrendous.'

He stared wildly around the room, and his gaze fixed upon Harriet, who was staring at him like she had seen a ghost. He strode over to her. 'Am I too late?' he demanded.

Baffled, she shook her head; and he let out a groan of relief and sank to one knee before her, right there in front of everyone!

Harriet looked as if she might faint.

'I've been an unconscionable idiot,' stated Mr Pringle. 'Harriet Blackburn, I love you with all my heart. Will you do me the great honour of becoming my wife?'

Harriet let out a whimper of joy. 'Yes, I will! Thank you!' she said very quickly and very loudly, then burst into tears. Evan leapt to his feet, held her hand tightly, and beamed at everyone.

Amidst all ensuing hugs, kisses, and congratulations for the happy couple, I could not help whispering to Jane, 'I can hardly believe it—Mr Pringle finally grew a backbone!'

'Yes,' Jane whispered back. 'Though I suspect it may also

be because I sent him an anonymous letter about Harriet's impending engagement—fictitious of course ...'

I chuckled and shook my head. 'Jane, one day, that quill of yours will get you into trouble.'

Jane smiled indulgently and touched my cup of tea with her own. 'Indeed.'

Chapter 21

One Year Later in Derbyshire

Dawn was breaking as I padded over to the thick purple velvet drapes and drew one back, letting in a shard of white light. The fires had not yet been lit, and the parquet floor was painfully cold to my warm feet. I scrunched my toes as I peered out the window.

'What are you doing, Fliss?' Max mumbled sleepily from the depths of our goose-feather eiderdown.

'I thought I heard horses,' I whispered to him. 'Go back to sleep.'

He yawned. 'They will be some hours away yet. I have made that trip many times, and there is always cause for delay. I would not expect them until late afternoon.'

Disgruntled, I let the drape fall into place, plunging our bedroom into darkness again. No doubt I was hearing imaginary clopping because I wanted Jane and Cassie to arrive this instant.

Padding back to bed, I slipped into the cosy warmth,

placing my icy feet on Max's warm calf to thaw out. He sucked in a breath. 'You are in for a walloping now, my lady!' he growled, gathering me roughly into his arms. I let out a soft squeal; he always said that, but he usually ended up doing nothing worse than smothering me with kisses. Max's bark was most definitely worse than his bite, as he had said—something I had come to learn for myself during our first year of marriage.

But I also could not help provoking him any chance I got, for I knew he secretly enjoyed my teasing; and it typically roused him to the point that he wanted to make love, which was pleasurable for us both. Due to the volatile nature of our physical relationship, Max kept a ready stock of French letters in his bedside table, also in the desk in his study and some in the side table in the parlour, as sometimes passion overcame us without warning; and we did not want to have to run up two flights of stairs to the bedroom and interrupt the moment.

We tried to be discreet, but living in a modest-sized mansion required several servants, and I was sure that if they ever pressed an ear to the parlour or study door, they would hear things that would make them blush! However, I had never caught any of them doing so, and they were adept at turning a blind eye to our dalliances. So I never felt embarrassed. Max had also made sure there were sturdy locks on the doors of the rooms we frequented so we were not caught in the act.

For the past week, Harriet and Evan had also been staying with us, so we had had to confine our romantic inclinations to the privacy of the bedroom and after everyone had retired in the evening. But they were ensconced in the opposite wing of the house, at least, so one couple did not have to worry about disturbing the other in the throes of passion.

And now Jane had accepted an invitation to visit with Cassie, and they were staying for three whole weeks! They had planned to come in spring. But it had been a wet season, and the weather had made the roads treacherous. Jane and I had written to each other, of course, but it was not the same as speaking directly. So I couldn't wait for them to get here.

Max squeezed my behind, which I always pretended not to like (but actually did immensely); and after an enjoyable tussle, along with a profusion of kisses on my lips, he released me with a sigh.

'I suppose we should not continue. We will need to rise for breakfast shortly.'

'Yes, I suppose,' I agreed, reluctantly removing my wandering hands from the depths of his nightshirt.

Having now nothing to do with them, I fidgeted.

'I wish they would arrive. I hate waiting!'

Max kissed the tip of my nose.

'I know, dearest, and you are doing well for someone who is terribly impatient. Luckily, it is one of the traits I love most about you. Otherwise, you would drive me to distraction.'

I propped myself up on my elbow and stared at him. In the gloom, I saw his lips curving into a smile. I traced them with a finger, then rubbed my hand along the scruff of his jaw, and he kissed my palm.

'You love my impatience? That is very odd.'

'And your impetuousness, intelligence, and intuitiveness.'

'So only words beginning with *I*?'

Max chuckled. 'I can go through the whole alphabet if you like. It will not be a chore to list all the things I love about you.'

I snuggled up against him. 'Well, you could start with *A* to *D* before breakfast ...'

'As you wish ...' But before he could begin, I distinctly heard the sound of carriage wheels crunching on the drive outside and sat up at once.

'They are here!' I exclaimed, whacking Max's arm excitedly.

'It seems I was entirely wrong then,' he said drolly.

'It is not the first time, and it will not be the last,' I

retorted with a laugh. 'Oh, I need to get dressed!'

Flinging back the covers, I scrambled out of bed and ran to the wardrobe. Grabbing the first gown I saw, I threw it on. Dragging my fingers through my long hair, I twisted it up and stuffed pins into it haphazardly while Max looked on, bemused.

'Slow down. They will not expect you to be up at this hour. Bertram can show them to their rooms.'

'No, I want to be there to greet them,' I panted, throwing him a kiss and racing out the door.

Jane and Cassie had already alighted from their carriage and were removing their travelling gloves in the entranceway when I pelted down the stairs and squealed in delight upon seeing them.

Jane turned. 'Flissy!' she cried, holding out her arms.

I ran over and embraced my friend tightly and then Cassie too, losing quite a number of hairpins in the process.

'I have been quite beside myself waiting for you to arrive!' I exclaimed. 'I was not expecting you until this afternoon, though.'

Jane winced. 'Please excuse the early arrival, but we stayed at lodgings nearby last night. So it was just a short journey this morning, and we did not want to waste another second. We have not even breakfasted.'

'Excellent,' I said, smiling at her. 'We will have some

now, and then we can do a tour of the estate.'

'Your description of the house did not do it justice,' Jane said, gazing up at the chandelier hanging from the ceiling.

'Well, I'm not a wordsmith like you,' I said, wrinkling my nose at her.

'How many bedrooms are there?' asked Cassie.

'Ten. Some are rather small, though, and hardly warrant the description. We have put you in the rooms facing the garden. So you can rest there for a few hours if you wish.'

'Rest?' said Jane. 'Oh no, just give us a cup of tea and toast, and we will be quite refreshed and ready to gaze at the splendid sights.'

'Speaking of "splendid sights",' muttered Cassie, and I turned to see Max descending the staircase with a dignified air. He had obviously decided to follow my example and personally greet our guests. He was wearing a smart well-fitting day suit, one of the several that he had commissioned from Papa after the wedding. He was the epitome of a handsome country gentleman, albeit with stubble as he had not had time to shave. Though I was used to his distinguished appearance, he was still a sight to behold at moments like this, and I noticed Jane and Cassie staring at him wide-eyed.

My husband, I thought proudly. Though I still considered the saying crass, I had to admit Aunt had been right in her estimation: I had most assuredly 'hooked' him.

Shortly afterwards, we were all gathered in the dining room for breakfast and partaking of the local pork sausages, which were tasty, crisp, and had been perfectly grilled. So tasty were they, in fact, that Evan, closely followed by Jane, had wolfed theirs down and were eyeing the silver dish on the table. The rest of us were being more decorous.

'Please do have another helping,' I told them. 'There are plenty more sausages where those came from.'

'If you insist,' said Evan, immediately serving himself. 'I must say, the food in these parts is delicious, or perhaps it is the excellence of your cook.'

'She is very good,' I agreed. 'But I do miss Sue. She makes such lovely sponges.'

I caught Max's eye, and his lips twitched.

'Speaking of Steventon, when will you be back, Harriet?' asked Jane, forking another two sausages from the dish onto her plate and accompanying them with a buttered roll.

Evan and Harriet had been married the week after Max and me, and they were living at Ashbury Manor for the time being. Harriet had taken over Rosalind's parlour (since the lady had told Evan she could not foresee herself ever returning to Steventon), and she often invited Jane and Cassie over for tea (the common black kind). But she had not been there of late as they had been visiting Evan's various relations in London and Wales, and had then journeyed north to stay with us.

'We will return in May, after we take Papa on an excursion to the South Coast. I managed to persuade him, finally, to take a respite from work. The sea air and change of scenery will do him good. Aunt will come too, of course.'

Harriet and I exchanged a knowing glance. Aunt's preference for Papa was hardly a secret, and we were well aware that if he were to return her inclination, there would be another marriage to celebrate. But so far, it had not happened.

Just last night, Harriet and I had been talking about it as we relaxed in the parlour after supper with a sherry while our husbands played cards. 'Do you think she will win him?' I asked. 'She has had no luck so far, and it is not for want of trying.'

'I am not sure,' Harriet replied. 'Papa holds fast to Mama's memory, and Aunt is reminded of that every time she sees her portrait in the dining room. We will see what happens. If we are away from Steventon and Papa has his guard down, she may have a chance. But I am staying well out of it and will do nothing to intervene even if she asks me to!'

The subject at the breakfast table now moved on to what the day held. Max and Evan were going fishing for trout, while us ladies planned to walk around the estate to take some fresh air and exercise.

'Dearest, how will you and Evan occupy yourselves after your fishing?' I enquired.

Max shrugged. 'We can go riding, or we might visit the village establishment for luncheon and a cold pint or two. Why? What will be happening here that you require our absence?'

'Nothing at all, my love,' I said innocently. 'We will just be relaxing and taking tea after our walk. Perhaps indulging in the odd bit of gossip—that sort of thing.'

Max pretended to shudder. 'We will make sure to be gone for the entire day then,' he said teasingly, and I stuck out my tongue at him while everyone laughed.

'You two are adorable,' said Jane after we had left the dining room to prepare ourselves for our walk. 'Max is even more smitten with you than when you were engaged, if that is possible.'

'Oh no, it is all an act. He despises me really but cannot escape because we are now stuck with each other,' I joked.

Jane scoffed in disbelief.

'Dear, I was there in the church when my father read you your vows. I did not think Max was even listening. It looked to me like he was musing intently on what was to happen that night *after* the ceremony.'

I giggled and linked my arm with hers. 'I have missed you. You say such deliciously wicked things. I cannot wait to hear your news.'

Jane smirked.

'Well, you have heard most of it in my letters. But I have been busy with something else in your absence, something that I think you might enjoy.'

The day was fine and mild, and we spent a pleasant two hours wandering around the estate, which was of an entirety of one thousand acres and included a lovely wood at the borders. Jane and Cassie exclaimed at intervals about the size of the land. I, in turn, insisted that it was not really *that* large in comparison to some estates and only *seemed* to be so because we were on foot and not in a carriage.

The tour finished with a visit to the stables to look in on George, who had accompanied me here. Papa had bestowed him to me as a wedding present and then immediately went and purchased a more obedient horse. But I did not mind having him here; and George was happy as the stables were roomy, he was well fed, and he enjoyed us going out on rides with Max and Apollo. Max had attempted to give him some training, but it was not proceeding well and often ended with Max red in the face from trying not to lose his temper. Privately, I thought it best if he left him alone. He was a free spirit like me and could not be tamed. But I would wait until Max reached that conclusion himself.

After our excursion, we spent the afternoon in the parlour, reclining on the sofas in our stockinged feet, drinking tea (and a little champagne), eating cakes, and reminiscing about Steventon with much laughter and enjoyment. I loved Max with all my heart and adored our life together, but it was marvellous to be amongst female company again.

When the afternoon drew to a close, Cassie and Harriet decided to rest in their rooms before supper, leaving Jane and me to our own devices. I took up a book I had been reading, and Jane ran off to collect her writing slope.

'Flissy, do you have any spare ink? I'm about to run out,' she said upon re-entering. 'Is there some in there?' She headed for the side table in the corner.

'Do not open that drawer,' I said abruptly, knowing it had a pile of French letters in it. 'It has some ... private documents. I will ring for one of the maids to fetch you some from the study.'

Jane arched an eyebrow but did not question me. 'Very well,' she said, settling herself at the table.

'Are you writing to someone?' I asked.

'Ah, no. I am making corrections to a ... manuscript.'

'Oh?'

She reached into her writing slope and brought out a bundle of paper.

'I have written a sort of novel,' she said, sounding nervous. 'I started with jottings but began writing it seriously after you left Steventon.'

Jane touched the title page almost reverently, and a jolt of understanding went through me. I knew what this was— after all, I had unwittingly glimpsed its conception in her parlour the night I had twisted my ankle. Now it was an actual book!

'I thought you might like to read it,' she continued. 'After all, it is based on you.'

'Me?' I said, trying to sound sufficiently surprised.

She nodded. 'I hope you do not take offence.' She bit her lip and looked worried. 'I may have borrowed quite heavily from your romance with Max.'

Indeed! But I shook my head to reassure her. 'I cannot imagine I will be offended. Has Cassie read it?'

Jane nodded. 'Several times.'

'All right, shall I read it now?'

'Yes, and I will write a letter to Mama while you do so to let her know we have arrived safely.'

I rang for a maid to fetch Jane some ink and took up the manuscript, which was titled *First Impressions*, with some trepidation, slightly worried that Max's night of drunken debauchery had made its way to her ears. But I need not have worried; the story, as it stood, was brilliant—funny, heart-warming, and perceptive, as well as having many tender moments and a host of entertaining characters.

Along with the Bennet family and the main romantic characters of lively Elizabeth and dour Mr Darcy, there were others I instantly recognised, including a ridiculous clergyman called Mr Collins. There was one scene in particular featuring him proposing to Lizzy, which set me off into a fit of giggles.

'Oh, Jane,' I said, heaving a deep breath and wiping my eyes. 'You have done my cousin's proposal justice indeed.'

'You do not mind?'

'No, not at all. I am flattered you have considered it comical enough to write about. And indeed, seeing it put like this, it very much is!'

'Keep reading,' she urged, and I did so with much enthusiasm until I came to the last page and its lovely conclusion. I heaved a satisfied sigh.

'It's wonderful!' I told her, and Jane grinned at me.

'You will see that I have made enough of a departure from the truth so everything is not too recognisable,' she said eagerly, more willing to talk about her book now that she knew I was not going to be angry. 'Note as well that I have given you three extra sisters.'

'Yes, and a mother!'

Jane looked sheepish. 'Well, I remembered you once said you wanted a mother so much that you would even take one that got on your nerves. So here is one that will do that admirably.'

Cheeky minx, I thought with a smile. 'Yes, Mrs Bennet is most definitely irritating,' I said. 'And Mr Collins is worse. I do not think Mr Humbleton would find it funny, though I see you have given him a wife!'

'Yes, Charlotte Lucas for plot purposes. But his ending is not as happy as Lizzy's,' she replied.

'That is true. I also see you used some of the descriptions I wrote you of our house for Mr Darcy's Pemberley and that the lake and trout feature. Max would be pleased. He loves fishing, as you know.' I handed her back the manuscript carefully. 'Thank you for letting me read it. I feel quite honoured!'

Jane smiled and inclined her head. 'I will keep refining it to make it better, and I feel the title needs to be changed. *First Impressions* is quite dull,' she said thoughtfully.

'What else would you have?'

'I am not sure. I was contemplating *Pride and Piglets* and adding Mr Darcy saying he thought a piglet was more attractive than Elizabeth,' she said.

I screwed up my face, a little pained at the remembrance

of Max saying that.

'Actually, on second thought, I will not put that in,' she said hastily, seeing my expression. 'I will think of another title.'

'Thank you,' I said, much relieved. 'Have you written any other stories?'

'Yes, a tale about three sisters that get thrown out of their house by their half-brother and have to live in a cottage in near poverty. I have added a dashing gentleman or two into the mix for the romance aspect.'

I clapped excitedly. 'Oooh, I love a good romance! Can I read it?'

She smiled tolerantly. 'Not yet. It needs reworking as it is currently in letter format, but I think it will work better as a narrative.'

'Well, I would love to read it once you have finished. Who knows, perhaps one day, you will get your manuscripts published and be a real author like Ann Radcliffe!'

'Perhaps,' Jane said quietly in her typical unassuming manner. But I could tell by her bright eyes and the determined set of her chin that becoming a published author was something she desired deeply. Strangely, at that moment, I was certain that she would achieve her dream because once Jane put her mind to something, there was no stopping her. I had a feeling in the years to come that I would indeed be honoured that my life had amused Miss Austen enough for her to write about it and even more so for taking my happy ending in hand. Max and I (or, should I say, Mr Darcy and Lizzy) would be forever grateful to her for that.

The End

Thank you for reading *Amusing Miss Austen,*
I hope you enjoyed it as much as I did writing it! If so,
I'd be thrilled if you left a review or star rating on Amazon
and/or Goodreads. Your feedback truly makes a difference
and helps this indie author's journey immensely.

Pick Up A Freebie!

Want more of Felicity and Max?

Join my mailing list using the link below and get exclusive bonus content sent to your email.

To join, type this address into your browser

eepurl.com/idcoHb

I'll keep you up to date with new releases and special offers. I promise I won't pass on your email or spam you.

Also by Angela

POX

Brontë Lovers

The Holly Project

You Had Me at Ice Cream

I'll Meet You in Florence

The House of Dating Disasters

My Double Life

Travel & Mayhem

3 Book Rom-Com Collection

All books available on Amazon and Kindle Unlimited

Acknowledgements

I'm so grateful for having a team of people to help me on the publishing journey. Thank you to my beta readers, Katharen Martin, Sarah Williamson, and Joanna Woollcombe-Gosson, for your insights and encouraging comments. Big thanks also to my diligent copyeditor Peachy Yap and to My Lan Khuc Valle for your gorgeous cover art. Last, but not least, thanks to my partner Chris Lambert, for reading my first draft and laughing in all the right places.

Check out the *Amusing Miss Austen* Spotify playlist at

➔ angelapearse.pub/book-spotify-playlists

To find out about my upcoming releases and special offers, sign up to my newsletter

➔ angelapearse.pub

About the Author

ANGELA PEARSE writes quirky romantic comedies that capture the humour of everyday life. A freelance editor with an MA in English, she enjoys travelling, hiking, cooking, binge-watching Netflix, and reading copious amounts of chick lit. Originally from New Zealand, Angela currently lives in Edinburgh with her partner. Visit angelapearse.pub.

Milton Keynes UK
Ingram Content Group UK Ltd.
UKHW041520080924
447929UK00008B/52